From the Vineyards of Hell

When ex lawman Captain Joshua Beaufort, late of Hood's Texas Brigade, marches clear of the hell that was Gettysburg he has no intention whatsoever of any further engagement in the Civil War; he has, in his own words, killed enough Yankees. But the war has not finished with the Confederate captain and, captured by Union troops, he is given a choice – help to end the war on their terms or spend the rest of it in a prisoner-of-war camp. Colonel Horatio Vallance and the mysterious E.J. Allen persuade him it is in his best interests to cooperate with the North. So, in company with and under the watchful eye of young Corporal Benbow, Beaufort returns to his home state of Texas to old loves, old friends and old enemies. His task, to bring back the head of Buford Post, a notorious warmonger and gunrunner who is in possession of 300 stolen Henry repeating rifles. . . .

From the Vineyards of Hell

Harry Jay Thorn

A Black Horse Western

ROBERT HALE

© Harry Jay Thorn 2017
First published in Great Britain 2017

ISBN 978-0-7198-2194-3

The Crowood Press
The Stable Block
Crowood Lane
Ramsbury
Marlborough
Wiltshire SN8 2HR

www.bhwesterns.com

Robert Hale is an imprint
of The Crowood Press

*With thanks to Toby, Harriet and Chris
and to my many friends who raised me up
when I had fallen.*

Typeset by
Derek Doyle & Associates, Shaw Heath
Printed and bound in Great Britain by
CPI Group (UK) Ltd, Croydon, CR0 4YY

PROLOGUE

The two boys were proud of their new ill-fitting butternut-grey uniforms and of their new Richmond rifles issued with bayonet, powder box and shot. They listened intently that warm July afternoon to the young captain, walking the long line, his sword shining in the afternoon sun, a red plume in his low-crowned hat. The plume was moving in the gentle breeze that brought with it the smell of the cooking-fires behind the long grey ranks of men.

'We may not be back in time for dinner, boys,' the captain said with a smile, 'but we will be back in time for supper though, if them Billy Yanks do not delay us. We would not want to miss two meals today, would we, boys?'

'No, sir, we would not want that.' The young pair joined in the cheerful reply, laughing.

'Then let us get the job done early, boys. Walk the field with me, fix your bayonets hard and tomorrow we may eat our breakfasts in Washington when we have shown these Yankees what Southern boys can do.'

Then, 'Are you with me, boys?' he yelled again, and once again they responded to a man.

'Then drummer boys and pipers to the front, colours to fore, and with Dixie in our ears we will walk right through them blasted Federals and they will curse the day we met here on this field in Manassas. Remember the name, boys, the name to tell your children; you tell them we were all here together at Manassas.

'Now let me hear a noise, a Rebel yell, boys, to let them Yankees know we are a' coming. Forward yo!

So they walked that field, men and boys, self-assured, invincible. Then they yelled and broke into a run, straight into the cannon, the rifle and the musket of the regrouped Union Army. Many fell that day to the shot and shell and the captain lost his hat and then his head, as did the drummer boy and the pipers all, and the colours fell. Then the field itself was alive, moving beneath their young feet and they trembled as the earth trembled and suddenly they were no more, gone in the blink of an eye, a flash of gunpowder and canister and no ground beneath their feet. There was no time for 'goodbye, Tom,' or 'goodbye, Luke.'

That was at Manassas, a place the Yankees called Bull Run.

CHAPTER ONE

GETTYSBURG

After a short while I no longer heard the thunder of the Union cannon or the zipping of the Minié balls as they creased the air around me or the Rebel yells of my boys as they marched behind me and up the gentle hill before us. Their yelling and screaming blended into one deafening roar as I marched, revolver in hand and my sword on my shoulder, towards the Federals at their railed fence. My grey uniform was drenched with the blood and the shredded flesh of the dying soldiers around me, for their bodies were pulverized by cannon and musket fire when, sometimes, a single cannon-round shredded and tore the hearts and souls from five or six men at one time, spraying their young bodies into the warm early-July afternoon.

All around me my boys fell, to the left and to the right; the gaps were quickly filled by more marching men with empty musket and fixed bayonet at the ready. The deafening sound numbed my ears and muffled into a single note, becoming a cadence in my head as I marched forward as if on a distant parade-ground square: *left right, left right, left right,* no longer seeing the enemy, so dense was the powder smoke that followed their fusillade and cloaked my tear-filled eyes.

A breeze, a wisp of a draught cleared the air before me and I gazed almost stupefied into the faces, only yards in front of me, of young, smoke-blackened men in blue uniforms who were as startled as I: staring and afraid. I raised my revolver and at arm's length cocked and discharged the piece of all six lead-filled paper cartridges into their line; then I turned and, sword still at arms, I walked through the dead, the wounded and the dying and made my way back down the hill, duty done.

Joseph P. Morgan was leaning against a live oak, its leaves blown away by cannon fire as if autumn had come early to the field, the branches splintered.

'Bad?' he asked, his voice coming through bloodless lips, husky and resigned.

'Very bad,' I said, revolver still in hand and sword still at arms. 'I believe I may have lost them all.'

'Are you going back up?'

'No, never. I will not walk that hill again.'

'Nor I,' he said, looking down at his leg.

His left leg was gone at the knee; the ragged, bloody ruins of his butternut-grey uniform trouser-leg were now matted with blood and splinters of bone.

'It doesn't hurt me now, it is numb. It did at first but the tourniquet stopped the bleeding and a corpsman gave me some laudanum, so I no longer feel or care. I need to rest a while.'

I set my sword against the live oak, holstered my revolver, carefully buttoned the flap and fished in my bag for a small pouch of tobacco and a short clay pipe. I stoked the bowl with the last of my rich, dark-brown tobacco and fired it, taking a deep draw before passing it to Morgan. He nodded gratefully.

'Bobby Lee has a lot to answer for this day.' The muttered words came filtered through a cloud of exhaled smoke.

'It was never achievable; I believe Longstreet and Pickett both knew that,' I said.

'Feeling's coming back, Josh, it hurts like hell.' He handed me back the warm pipe and I tapped it clean on my boot top.

'Give me your arm, Joseph,' I said; then, after picking up my sword, I reached for him and together we made our way down to the clearing where blood-soaked men gathered together, some praying for death, others praying for life. Surgeons bustled around, stretcher-bearers formed an almost continuous antlike line to the hastily erected tents. Walking wounded helped where they could and fires sprang up everywhere, the smoke of green wood was scented with the aroma of burnt coffee beans. It was quieter there than on the hill but my ears still rang from the distant cannonade.

Two elderly men stepped forward and relieved me of my burden, carefully laying Joseph Morgan on to a stretcher.

'We will take him now, son; get yourself some coffee.' Gentle voices, Virginians I guessed. As they carried him away he looked back once and said:

'What now, Joshua?'

He deserved an answer and I hope he heard it.

'I'm going home now, Joseph, and I am never coming back.'

The wounded man offered a pain-racked smile.

'Come visit me in Modesty, we'll sit a spell, share a pipe, sing "Lorena" once again and talk about old times. Will you do that, Josh?'

'I'll see you there, Joseph, I promise.'

I waved him goodbye and, with sword still at the shoulder, I marched slowly out of that bloody clearing in the wooded grassy fields of Gettysburg and made my long way back to Texas. I never made it, not that time. For me that journey ended a day later in a green field where one of Chamberlain's 20th Maine ran me down and cracked open my noggin with the barrel of his empty pistol.

Joseph Percival Morgan watched as his friend Joshua Beaufort vanished into the distant tree line and the stretcher-bearers carried him into a large tent. There a surgeon in a blood-soaked apron gave him a cursory check and instructed the two men to set him on the table, which was, like his apron, red with the blood of his previous patients. The air was acrid with the bitter metallic stink of blood new and old. Two men held his shoulder down while the surgeon removed what was left of his left leg just above the knee. With only a hickory stick gripped between his teeth to dampen the pain a dark cloud enveloped him and he drifted off into a world of noise and confusion.

CHAPTER TWO

COLONEL HORATIO VALLANCE

I have been coldcocked before; waking up from a nowhere place was not new to me. First comes an awareness of life but not a sense of when or where you are and then, very slowly at first, a realization that you are a living person on a journey back from a faraway place, a place of darkness. My head hurt, throbbed, but not with an unbearable pain: a welcome reminder that I was alive. I was lying on a narrow cot covered in a white sheet. I turned my head to the left and to the right and could see that I was on part of a long line of cots, all covered from top to toe with blood-stained white sheets. An orderly stepped forward, followed closely by a Union soldier with two chevrons and a shoul-dered carbine. The orderly was a tall, thin, red-haired man with a sallow face, a sad face enlivened only by his piercing blue eyes.

'Don't worry, son, they are all dead but you are not. The colonel decided that you should be, though, and thought this was the place for you.' His voice had a soft hint of the

Irish to it.

'I need a piss,' I said.

'You have had several already but we have cleaned you up some. You have been here three days; we were not sure if it was a concussion or exhaustion and opted for the latter.'

I raised the sheet and looked. Apart from my grey socks lovingly knitted for soldiers by the good ladies of Richmond, I was buck naked.

'Three days?' I queried.

'And a bit, around eighty hours all told.' He turned to the corporal. 'Bring the captain the clean clothes Colonel Vallance sent over.'

The soldier dumped a small pile of clothes on the bottom of the cot: a clean Union-blue shirt, an undershirt, a pair of clean drawers and a pair of pants, butternut-grey with yellow piping.

'Thank you, Corporal,' I said. He touched his cap in a sort of a salute.

'You are welcome, sir.'

'Sir?' I said.

'Colonel Vallance tells us to treat all officers with respect, blue or grey; insists upon it, he is very strict about that. When the captain is ready he would like me to escort you over to his tent.'

He was a tall, fair-haired young man, so clean-shaven that I wondered whether he was old enough to grow whiskers. His voice was soft, almost warm, but his eyes were a cold pale blue, alert, and although his carbine was held loosely I had no doubt he could and would use it if need be.

'He would?'

'Yes, sir, he would – and in fact he insists on that also.'

I looked at the orderly with an unasked question on my

12

lips, but he answered before I could speak.

'Up to you, son. Short of a headache I guess you are OK but best take it slow. Try sitting up first, that's the hard part, then take it from there.'

He was right; sitting up was the hard part. My head swam, I felt giddy and nauseated, but these sensations quickly subsided and after a few minutes I swung my naked legs out from under the sheet and settled them on the plank floor. I tried to stand erect, but tottered; the orderly stepped forward and steadied me, holding my arm as I pulled on the drawers and the pants. They were a snug fit.

'They fit good,' I said quietly.

'The colonel was an undertaker before the war; he is a pretty good judge of that sort of thing; knows just how tall and wide you are without the aid of a tape-measure.' He smiled, gave me his arm and said, 'Let's give it a try, shall we?'

'I need some boots,' I said.

'Dead men's boots we have a-plenty, there is a heap of them over there.' He indicated a large pile of footwear. 'Choose a pair likely to fit but be careful there isn't a foot in them; it happens we miss one now and then.'

A battlefield sense of humour or the truth? I could not be sure, but I selected a pair of empty short-topped boots that seemed to fit snugly over my socks.

I leaned heavily on his arm for a while. As we passed the lines of sheet-covered cots I noticed that where there should have been two feet protruding there was often only one; sometimes none at all. I made no comment, but as we emerged into the bright daylight the gentle breeze and the freshness of the air was welcome. We passed several long tents on our journey, with the ever-watchful young corporal at our rear. Once we passed a work group of bloody-aproned soldiers loading body parts, mostly legs and arms, on to a wheeled cart; they showed no sign of noticing our passing. Within a little while I was able walk without the aid of the orderly's strong shoulder. We paused at the entrance of a small tent while the corporal stepped ahead and raised the flap.

'Luck to you, soldier,' the orderly said. 'Next time, be sure to wake up dead. It has to be a better place than this.' He smiled. I watched him till he was out of sight before allowing the corporal to usher me into the tent.

The inside of the tent was not what I expected: no grand battlefield accoutrements, just a bare fold-up wooden table, three canvas-backed field chairs and two people. One of these last stood in a shadowed corner of the tent; lamplight glinted off his wire-framed spectacles. The other was an officer in the full dress uniform of a colonel in the Union Army; he was already seated at the table which was bare except for a leather-bound folder. He stood up and offered me his hand. There is no denying that war is a strange affair. I took the hand, receiving a firm handshake from the man who had in all probability been trying to blow me away on Cemetery Ridge or Little Round Top only days before.

'Horatio Vallance at your service, sir. Welcome to my headquarters, such as they are.'

His was another voice tinged with the Irish. He was a tall thin man with a mop of red hair and a neatly trimmed goatee on a handsome rosy-cheeked face. He indicated the single chair and I took it gratefully, my legs were beginning to falter either through lack of exercise, food, water or a combination of all three.

'Would you care for a coffee or something stronger?' he offered.

'Coffee would be fine,' I said, wondering what the hell

was going down in that tent only fifteen or so miles from the Gettysburg battlefield where so many of my – and, I guessed, his – companions had fallen.

'Three mugs of Joe if you please, Corporal, and on the double; this man looks about done in.' The soldier set his carbine within reaching distance of Vallance and slipped silently out of the tent. Vallance turned to me and sat on one of the two remaining chairs.

'No sugar or milk, I am sorry to say; not a live cow within miles and your boys have seen to it that sugar is in short supply.'

'Good to know they did something useful today,' I said.

'It was bloody three days and it will get worse as the war goes on.'

'Why am I here? Why not in a prisoner-of-war camp? I hear you have them,' I said.

'You are here because you interest me,' he replied. 'They caught you marching through the trees, your sabre at your shoulder and a pistol in your hand. Lucky they did not shoot you, but I understand the trooper you ran across was out of powder. If you would prefer a prisoner-of-war camp it can be arranged.'

'This will do fine – and by the way, thanks for the clean clothes. What happened to my old ones?'

'To be frank with you, Captain, they stank. They were covered in blood and brains and later in shit and piss. We thought you might be better off without them and in any case they have likely been burned now, along with bits of both your and my own comrades.'

'And my trappings, you burned them as well?'

'Your personal belongings and your shoulder bag are here. Would you like them?'

'I would like my makings.' I said, trying to hide my irritation.

Vallance walked over to where the man in the shadows was standing and came back with my leather shoulder bag. He tossed it on to the table. I did not check the contents but removed my pipe and tobacco and stared glumly at the empty pouch, remembering my last shared smoke with Joseph Morgan in the woods below Cemetery Ridge.

The young corporal returned with a tin tray bearing three cups of steaming coffee. He placed them on the table, picked up his carbine and withdrew, closing the tent flap behind him. Vallance placed two of the cups on the table and took the other to the silent man in the corner. I sipped the coffee; it was hot and burned my mouth but it was welcome, even without sugar.

'Here, try some of my tobacco, dark and the best Virginia has to offer. There is a certain irony there, would you not think?' He tossed a small leather pouch towards me.

'They do say to the victor the spoils,' I said, tamping the fresh moist tobacco into the bowl of my clay pipe. I accepted a box of blue-top matches from him. So civilized, so far away from the cannons' roar of yesterday: two soldiers sitting down, shooting the breeze.

'You will forgive me, sir,' I said, blowing smoke out through my open lips, which still burned a little from the hot coffee, 'but I do not believe you got me here, washed me down and dressed me up so that we could share pleasantries over tobacco and hot coffee.' I did not hide the annoyance I felt but he merely smiled and leaned back in his chair.

'You are so right, I did not, Joshua Beaufort, late of Hood's Texas Brigade, but I do wonder what you were doing with Pickett at the Ridge when your comrades were elsewhere. Did you have a sudden desire to join the infantry?'

'Your men shot two horses out from under me and there were no remounts, so I followed the cannon and marched with Pickett. A lot of us did, but you know that already: they were littered all over your field.'

Vallance studied me for a long moment.

'Yes, I knew that. Truth to tell, I watched you march up that slope; we all did. Sometimes you vanished in a cloud of smoke, then re-emerged, revolver still in your hand and your sabre at your shoulder. You kept coming, vanishing and coming on again. Then quite suddenly you walked out of the smoke not ten yards from where I was standing, emptied your weapon into my men, killing at least two of them before waving the sword around your head, giving out that damned yell, turning and marching back the way you came.

'We fired volley after volley at you and you vanished from our view. Later, when the killing was over, I walked that same route expecting to find your body, only to have you turn up a day later as a prisoner of war. I am notified of any Confederate officer so taken and I recognized you immediately.'

'I remember nothing of that, Colonel, not a thing.' It was true, I had no recollection of marching up to Cemetery Ridge.

'Damnedest thing I ever saw. In my army you would get a medal, but as the Confederacy does not set too much store in such fripperies you will at least get a mention in dispatches – if such things are given to deserters. You were deserting, were you not?'

I smiled across at him.

' "Skedaddled", we say, but it amounts to the same thing, I suppose.'

He opened the leather folder and read the top page of a dossier before closing it again.

'Joshua Beaufort, age 42 years, Captain in Hood's Texas Brigade. Before the war you ran horses in the Windy Ridge, Texas border country with your father, a Virginian, and your two younger brothers. You served as a part-time deputy sheriff in Pueblo County with a growing reputation for being better than most with a handgun. You were numbered among the personal friends of Sam Houston with political aspirations of your own, and when he quit over a belief you shared: that of not wishing to sign the agreement of cessation, you also quit.

'You were not a slave owner and refused to fight for the Confederate cause. Your brothers enlisted and were both killed at Bull Run, the battle you call Manassas. You enlisted two months after the news of their passing reached Pueblo.'

He closed the folder and looked at me directly.

'Why then did you join the fight for the Confederacy when your heartfelt principles were against the breaking-up of the Union?'

He laid it flat for me there in that musty tent, which had the fairground smell of tobacco, dry earth and crushed grass.

'You missed a few things out, Colonel. My father went out to our red barn and shot himself with a .36 Navy Colt when news reached us that my brothers had been killed. My mother passed away of a broken heart shortly thereafter. Is that not in your report?'

I paused there for a moment, thinking about it; so much had happened since those far-off days but I knew the truth and it had to be said.

'I joined the army to kill Yankees and I have done a fair job of it so far.'

'So why quit now?'

'I've killed enough.' The answer to his question was

that simple.

You could have cut the long silence that followed with a knife. I waited. Vallance climbed to his feet, smiled sadly down at me.

'Perhaps, Captain Beaufort, it is time for some supper.' He nodded to the man in the corner and we left the dark tent together.

Supper in the officers' mess was a quiet affair of hushed conversations, not about the war but of the peace that would eventually follow. Our voices were, as were those of other officers present, muted. The flickering light from the oil lamps and the glow of the many campfires that were scattered among the bivouacked Northern army danced upon the canvas of the tent and gave the evening a feeling of a reality that was far beyond the grasp of these many men so immersed in war. We were at times the central topic of conversation: the Rebel captain with the Union colonel sharing a meal of boiled bacon, beans, coarse white bread and wine.

After supper and a final pipe Vallance gave me an ultimatum: I could go either to the prisoner compound or, if I gave him my parole that I would not attempt to escape, to a tent of my own with one guard: the silent corporal. I chose the latter and gave him my word that I would stay put. It was an easy choice to make, I was not in any fit shape to wander the fields of Pennsylvania even had I wanted to.

'Goodnight to you, Captain. Here,' he handed me his tobacco pouch, 'take this. I have more. We will resume our conversation over breakfast. Sleep well.'

I watched him, a tall straight man walking through the flickering darkness, returning a greeting or a salute here and there before the night took him. I smiled at the young corporal.

19

'Goodnight, son. Doze if you want to; I promise to stay put.'

He opened the flap of the one-man tent and stood to one side.

'Goodnight, sir.'

CHAPTER THREE

CORPORAL JACOB BENBOW

There is nothing in this world that can beat the good-morning greeting of frying bacon and, north or south of the Mason-Dixon line, it always smells the same, it has a worldly familiarity about it that stirs the juices and gives a man an appetite, makes him want to eat even if he is not hungry. Campfires were to the left and right of me and the smell of the frying rashers was unmistakable.

The corporal snapped to attention as I opened the flap and he handed me a towel and a wash cloth, saying:

'Compliments of Colonel Vallance, sir. I am to show you to the ablutions area.'

I stretched, stamped my feet and looked around me. Union soldiers were everywhere, as far as the eye could see; licking them would be near impossible.

'What is your name, son?'

He looked at me long and hard, wondering, I supposed, if it was OK to share such information with a Johnny Reb.

21

'Jacob Benbow, sir.' His voice was neither friendly nor cold, he seemed indifferent to my company: an order to be obeyed; whether he found the order distasteful or not I had no way of knowing.

'They call you Jake?'

'Mostly, sir, they call me Corporal.'

'Well, Corporal Jacob Benbow, you show me where I can take a dump and get a wash and then where that cooking bacon is at.'

The corporal raised the flap and closed it behind me. The inside of Vallance's tent was much the same as on my last visit, the three chairs, the shadowy man in the corner. There were a smoke-blackened can of hot coffee and two filled tin mugs on the table. The only difference was that this time there were two leather folders in front of the straight-backed colonel. He greeted me with what I considered to be a tired smile and indicated the chair opposite him.

'I trust you slept well, Captain?'

'Like a dead man, Colonel.'

'Good, then now resurrected and refreshed, I hope. I am not going to beat about the bush this morning, Captain Beaufort; we have both had long enough to size each other up, to know where we stand, so I am getting right to it.'

'That would be good,' I said, sipping the hot sweet coffee. 'You found some sugar; I never thought to taste it again.'

'I have the final tally – or as near as we can get – to the outcome of the fight here at Gettysburg.' He opened the leather folder, took out a sheet of paper, fished in his jacket pocket for a pair of wire-rimmed eyeglasses, hooked them on and read from the page.

'There were over fifty thousand casualties: dead, dying, wounded or missing. The score: you lost five thousand more men than we did. I have no idea of the number of horses killed but I do know that fifteen hundred artillery horses perished and, like the men, many of them are still out there, rotting where they fell. So much for war, sir, so much for victory, so much for Gettysburg.'

They were stunning numbers, I had no idea of the scope of the three-day fight, only of my tiny portion of it. I filled my pipe with his tobacco and my hands trembled as I lit the match and fired the bowl. The nicotine rush of the first intake of smoke made me giddy and the room revolved around me for a full minute, during which time neither of us spoke a word. I set the hot pipe down and picked up the tin coffee cup, sipped and waited as the moving things around me settled back into their rightful places.

'That was just one fight, Captain, one three-day engagement in a war that will go on and on unless someone, somehow, helps to shorten it. If hostilities are prolonged those figures I have just read out will seem as nothing to the final total – and there *will* be a final total: there always is. Would you be prepared to do something about that if it were within your power to do so?'

I thought about that for a long moment.

'The only thing I can do is to not add to it, I have nothing else to offer other than that I have laid down my arms.'

He studied me with care and, I sensed, with some concern. I realized I was weeping, the tears running down my cheeks and dripping into the coffee cup. He got to his feet and turned his back to me.

'I was as shocked as you are, sir, but I have not the time to weep; my job is to find a way or ways to shorten this war.

23

Yours, if you are willing, is to help me.' He turned back to face me. 'The Confederacy is doomed, Captain; the Union Army will march to the sea, Atlanta and Richmond will fall to our cannon. It is inevitable. We have the political will, the money, the manpower and the resources to triumph in the end, no matter how long it will take and how many will perish. How many of your company did you lose?'

He was hitting home, hitting where he knew it would really hurt me.

'At Little Round Top? That I do not know: most of them, I guess. Those who had their mounts shot from under them? That I do know. I led fifty-one men afoot to join Pickett at Cemetery Ridge and the only one I saw still standing after the fight was a man on a splintered left leg, shot off at the knee, leaning against a live oak. I shared a pipe with him before I left. He was also a Texan. God help us.' I rubbed my shirtsleeve across my eyes and stared at him long and hard, trying to read the man behind the uniform.

'I doubt that God is on either side in this bloody war; I doubt very much He wears butternut grey and I am certain He does not wear the Union blue, I believe it is up to us to end the conflict and reunite the Union as He intended it to be.'

'What do you expect of me and why me?'

'In part, this war is being prolonged and will continue to be so by men who have little or no interest in either of our causes but only an interest in making money. Unscrupulous profiteers, they will replace your fallen mounts, they will resupply you with munitions, provisions, muskets, cannon and shot, even the Henry repeating rifles that you Southerners so covet. All of that at a high cost, of course; there will always be those who will make money out of war. But it isn't only war materials they peddle;

above all they will fill your ranks with false hope for a cause that was lost the day you fired that first cannon shell on Fort Sumter.'

'And just who are these men and again, why me?'

'Simple answer really is: because you are a Texican, but let me introduce my colleague here.' He nodded to the shadow of the man in the corner. The man stepped into the light. He was tall, rotund, wearing civilian clothing that included a long black woollen jacket and pants to match. He had dark piercing eyes, a large nose and a long auburn beard which, combined with the equally thick moustache, hid his lips and most of his lower face.

'Major E.J. Allen, allow me to introduce you to Captain Joshua Beaufort, late of Hood's Texas Brigade.'

'At your service, Captain Beaufort.' His dark, deep, rich voice seemed to issue forth from the mass of red hair and the words, though softly spoken, unmistakably denoted a Scot. I got to my feet and took the offered hand. Another firm handshake. He seated himself on the chair next to Vallance – or rather, on the edge of its seat – and leaned forward, giving the appearance of a man on the move, a man ready to pounce at a second's notice.

I sat down again and waited.

'A good deal of the Confederate supplies are coming through Texas, much of it from south of the border, beyond the Rio Grande. You know that country and you know the people. Major Allen is forming a unit to counter these resuppliers, these warmongers who thrive on the misfortunes of others.'

'What unit is that, Major?' I looked directly at the burly Scot.

'The Union Intelligence Service, a kind of secret service formed to protect the Union either in peace or at times of war.'

I looked over at Vallance.

'I will not spy for you, Colonel—'

'Good God, man!' He interrupted me with a laugh. 'We don't need more spies. The South leaks like a sieve; we get intelligence from all over: from freed blacks, journalists, little old ladies in Richmond and double agents in Washington itself. We do not want or need information about the trafficking through Texas, we simply want it stopped. We believe that the unit the major here represents can do just that. We will take the Mississippi River and close that route but we need boots on the ground to cut the heads off those warmongers who feed the war at source.'

I studied the two Union men.

'What are my alternatives?'

'Alternative, Captain: it is singular. You either help end this war in the field, your loyalty to your fellow soldiers and your political belief shared with Houston intact, or you rot in a prisoner-of-war camp and the war goes on.'

It was not a difficult choice to make.

'I don't see what one man can do,' I said.

'Two men actually, but I will come to that. Sometimes a very few men can do what an army cannot and this is one of those times. I am not interested in horses or beans or even cotton; what I am interested in is the Henry repeating rifle.' He paused, studying me closely. 'Are you familiar with the Henry, Captain?'

'I am, sir. One of our company commanders owned such a rifle; trouble was, he couldn't replace the ammunition for the damned thing.'

Vallance laughed, filled his pipe and passed the tobacco pouch to me.

'Just as well; a gun like that in the hands of a man like you could win a battle. What do you know of it?'

Weapons of war were my thing; they were what you killed Yankees with, so I had learned about them quickly, sometimes the hard way.

'Sixteen-shot, seventeen if you are foolish enough to have one in the breech. No safety catch. .44-calibre, rim fire. It has been dubbed the rifle you could load on Sunday and shoot all week long.' I snapped out the words in the text-book staccato style I used for giving information to my men who needed to know, needed to learn. But Vallance already knew; he smiled at my lecture-room style.

'We heard that,' he said.

'Accurate up to around two hundred yards for a regular trooper,' I continued in the same rhythm, 'maybe even further for a crack shot, buff-hunter or the like.'

'A trained sharpshooter like Corporal Benbow here can take down a man at closer to four hundred yards and then some.' He turned and nodded to the young corporal. 'Put it on the table, son, but make certain it is empty.'

Benbow stepped forward and set a leather rifle case on the table, undid the fastening and slid out the Henry repeater. He pointed it to the ground, worked the lever and pulled the trigger. It snapped on the empty breech with a cold and deadly metallic click. He was giving a performance and I was the lone member of the audience. He set the gun squarely between us as I suspected he had been rehearsed to do, then stood back.

'That right – you can bring down a man at four hundred yards, Corporal?' Vallance asked.

'I can centre a target or a deer at that range – and better, sir, but I have never drawn down on a man.'

'Not even a Johnny Reb?'

'No, sir, not even a Reb.

Vallance turned back to me.

'Can you imagine what a unit of . . . say . . . fifty men

27

could do if armed with these beauties, North or South, blue or grey?'

'A lot of men would die,' I said quietly.

'You are damned right: a lot of men would die; a battle won, a battle lost and so it would go on.'

I made no comment but waited, drawing on my pipe, watching the performance.

'Now here's the rub, Captain. These weapons are in short supply and, like you say, ammunition is hard to come by for the South. The piece is not regular issue here in the north, although it is my belief that it should be but that is neither here nor there. What is important is the fact that three hundred Henry repeating rifles plus an untold amount of ammo has gone missing from the New Haven Armoury in Connecticut.

'We suspect they have made their way to Mexico, for sale to the highest bidder no matter what insignia he might wear. Your army or mine, a lot of dead young soldiers.' He paused.

'We want those rifles back lest they should fall into the wrong hands. You think about that for a moment.' He turned to Benbow. 'Thank you, Corporal Benbow, you and the Henry may stand down.'

The corporal stepped back to the table, gathered up the rifle and case and silently left the small smoke-filled tent to the three of us: the colonel, the major and the captain.

It really was something to think about and I did, long into that night. In the darkness of the dreams that inevitably came with sleep I saw a thousand young men fall to a fusillade of fire; some wore grey and some wore blue but their blood was red. I heard a chorus of *Dixie* and *The Battle Hymn of the Republic* and young voices from a long line of white-faced dead men singing *Lorena* as they marched along a granite-walled dirt road that led to nowhere.

A month later I rode out of the Union headquarters on a Yankee horse, in Union Army hand-me-downs, with a newly converted holstered Colt 1860 Army in an open-top high-ride holster on my hip, a Union Intelligence Service badge and identification sewn into the leather upper of a dead man's boot. I was accompanied, at the insistence of Vallance, by young Corporal Jacob Benbow, late of the 20th Maine.

Hidden deep in the leather of my saddlebag were documents showing undeniable proof that I was indeed Joshua Beaufort of Hood's Texas Brigade, rumoured missing or dead but actually very much alive and now transferred to the quartermaster's unit of the Army of Northern Virginia. That second identification would come into effect once we were clear of Union-held territory and were safely into Virginia. Vallance had assured me that both my own and Benbow's papers were in order, courtesy of a Union agent working in Lee's headquarters. True or not, we had to trust that assurance.

That had been two months ago, but that day at Gettysburg, of all the previous long days and months of the long and bloody Civil War, a war I rode, walked and toiled through without a single wound, sticks with me like a tick on a porcupine, an itch I can never reach and scratch. That sound and the stench of death envelop me like a shroud.

I am to become what I am to become: a hunter of men.

CHAPTER FOUR

TWO FOR TEXAS

It took us a hard-riding eight weeks to reach the Texas and Louisiana border, weeks of dodging both Union and Confederate soldiers. Mostly we rode at night by moonlight or starlight and always with an eye on our back trail. We changed horses many times and once took a brigantine along the coast, saving us many days and saddle sores. We ditched our army blues when we left Pennsylvania and entered the Confederate states of the once mighty Union.

The young corporal turned out to be a pleasant travelling companion, a well-spoken and educated soldier, quick to learn and easy on occasion to converse with. It was not difficult to see why he had risen so quickly from the ranks to earn his two chevrons, chevrons he insisted on cutting from his uniform before discarding it for a pair of Confederate-issue grey pants and tunic.

I thought long and hard about the final conversation I'd had with Vallance over pipes and fresh morning coffee. 'Texas is not a battle ground – nor likely to be,' he had said. 'I have the very real feeling that Texicans are citizens of Texas and that independence sticks to them like a tick to a dog. They are much happier to chaw on their tobacco and play cowboy than to ride off to a war that many of them, like you, have little interest in; it is a secret that they are happy to keep for fear of reprisals.

'Those who do fight are some of the bravest of the brave but I feel that they are fighting for Texas and not for the Confederacy. Lincoln is toying with the idea of setting up a garrison there to keep the warmongers from doing business with the Mexicans, but he is being advised against it. Men like you, sharing my beliefs, can do much more to bring an end to the conflict than a regiment of soldiers. You stir up Texas at your peril.'

He smiled, passed me his pouch and I refilled my pipe.

'Poke a Texan with a stick and he is liable to poke you back, Colonel.'

'Your papers are authentic, you are a procurement officer for the Confederacy's Quartermaster and the gold you carry is enough to convince any man who queries your intent. The map is the best we can do but I guess you know the country better than anyone. Head for your ranch on the Nueces and somewhere along the line you will meet up with one of Major Allen's officers. He will advise you on the situation locally. You will be looking to make contact with a man named Buford Post; he is the head of the serpent, kingpin of the money men down there.

'But be certain of this, Captain Beaufort, he is no Texan, he is not a patriot; the only cause he is fighting for is his own personal wealth, and every nickel, dime or dollar he makes filters its way back to Washington, where he invests it in munitions to keep the war going.

'That new Colt conversion you are wearing probably has his money behind the brass you load it with, and the Henry rifle you carry on your saddle was probably paid for through one business or another of his. The more men who die the richer he becomes.

'I wish you luck, sir, and look after that corporal of mine. I want him back here in one piece.'

'You are putting a lot of trust in your judgement of me.'

'Major Allen and I never make a mistake in our judgement of men; you may be tempted but you will not break your word to me, that I know. Should we be wrong, his organization will hunt you down and kill you.'

He smiled. There was no warmth in his words and he added just as coldly:

'Just bring me the head of Buford Post.'

Most of our long journey south was uneventful; we did not seek out confrontation or companionship with locals and we were often concerned for the perils of our long journey. In fact, on only one occasion did we engage a so-called enemy but that brief confrontation changed many things for both me and Corporal Benbow.

We had just entered Virginia, ditched our Federal blues, donned our Southern greys and set up a hot camp, so that after days of hardtack and corn dodgers we could eat an evening meal freshly cooked: a jackrabbit shot earlier that day by Benbow. The next morning, following a fair night's sleep in the open air and a good breakfast, I was about to load our pack animal when three men walked into our camp. I could smell them before I actually saw them: three men, filthy, unshaven, unwashed in beat-up clothing and dirty, raggedy dusters. They stood there staring at me; they were armed and unwelcome. The largest of the trio glared at me from beneath the crumpled brim of what once had been a fine derby hat. He smiled through his dark beard but the smile did not reach his dark eyes.

'A fine morning to be sure, sir.' The words were clipped

and sharp, he was definitely not a Virginian; a Jayhawker, I guessed, from just about anywhere.

'It was,' I said, 'until a few moments ago.'

'You got grub?'

'Not enough to share,' I said, moving away from the packhorse and carefully watching his two younger companions as they spaced themselves out, one on each side of him.

'They got grub, Gus. I can smell the bacon.' The youngest of the trio moved forward, sniffing the air like a dog. Seventeen or eighteen years old, I guessed, a smaller replica of the big man. He wore a beat-up derby hat cocked on the back of his greasy hair.

'Fine animals for a Johnny Reb to be riding,' the older man said, nodding to where the saddlehorses chomped on the dew-covered grass. 'Are you a deserter, a Texas yellow belly?" As he spoke he opened the duster wide, tucking the trailing, ragged material behind the holstered revolver. 'I can tell you're not from around here.' He looked down at our bedrolls beside the fire. 'Where's your friend at? He hunting or crapping?'

I did not answer but watched his right hand.

'Maybe we'll take them ponies; no call for us to be walking while you Rebs ride on them fine animals.' He grinned, his lips moist around rotted teeth. 'A sort of toll – yes, let's call it that: a fee for passing through Virginia.'

'Maybe you will not take the animals,' I said. As I spoke his hand began to move. I pulled and shot him in the chest. He reeled backwards. I crouched and shot the man on his left. The youngest of the three was in the fight then; he had just got off one quick ball in my direction when the Henry rifle cracked behind me and Benbow stepped clear of the trees. He was working the lever of the gun and he fired again from the hip.

The youngster twisted around under the impact of the lead and fell across the fire, sending a shower of sparks into the brisk morning air. I stepped forward and rolled him clear of the embers with my boot, at the same time stamping out the flames engulfing the tail of his long duster.

'Jesus Christ!' Benbow muttered, his voice not much more than a whisper.

'You will not find *him* in these woods this morning, Jake. By the way, that was fine shooting – on the move and from the hip.'

If he heard me he did not acknowledge the compliment and I wondered if it were the youngster's first action. I turned on my heel and moved to quieten the horses; they had been frightened by the fracas and were now fighting their hobbles. As I walked past the big man he tried to sit up, blood was dribbling over his rotten teeth and down his chin. He pointed a shaking finger at me as I passed. Without aiming I shot him in the temple and watched as he rolled back on to the damp earth.

Benbow stared at me.

'What?' I asked. 'You want me to heal him? I just killed the son of a bitch twice is all.' As I walked I punched out the empty brass from my new Colt and pushed in fresh rounds.

'Are we going to bury them?'

'No, *I* am not, but I will wait for you if you want to.'

'No, sir,' he shook his head, 'let's be going from this place.'

'First rule of the battlefield, boy: gather anything they have that will be of use to us. Take their sidearms and ammunition and knives, search them, see if they have any smoking tobacco, stogies, matches or liquor. Leave anything that identifies them though; maybe someone more

34

charitable than I will pass this way and give them the burial they do not deserve and probably did not want. I believe they were afoot, but I will check to see if there are any mounts near by.'

I tossed him an empty gunny sack for his findings and left him to it while I continued to load and saddle the horses and check the area beyond the trees in the direction from which the three had walked.

So we moved quietly on, putting as much ground between us and the dead Jayhawkers as was possible in a day's ride. I was thinking that I had learned two things: one of which was that young Jacob Benbow was handy with a gun and cool under fire but that he experienced a troubled aftermath. I had also learned something about myself. I had learned that unlike when killing, in the frantic heat of battle, men fighting in uniform for a given cause, for whom I could feel compassion, I could just as surely kill a man in cold blood and feel nothing for him. I had learned that I could only feel the fire in my own belly and my one saving grace was knowing that the fire lightened the darkness that I knew the youngster had seen in my eyes.

The surprise on the Jayhawker's face as my round struck him matched that evinced by my young companion as he watched, but I showed no surprise. I am no gunfighter, no exponent of the fast draw, but I am competent, steady and, above all, accurate. Faster guns than mine have fallen to a less worthy opponent because their accuracy did not match their speed.

We crossed the border by the Sabine River and rode into Texas, listening to the distant rumble of cannon fire as Texas artillery thwarted the Union's attempt to set up a garrison on the sovereign soil of the Lone Star State. The

Federals had been beaten back by determined sharp-shooters and deadly accurate artillery men.

Three more days saw us across the Nueces River south of Uvalde and just north of Del Rio on the Mexican border, in sight of the rolling green bottomland of the valley and the ranch I knew as the Rocking Lazy B. My father told us it stood for Lazy Bastard but my brothers and I knew different, that he had named it after our mother, Beatrice. The brand was a letter B with a half-moon under it as if it were asleep and rocking to the South Texas breeze.

We paused in the late morning on the slight rise to the north of the ranch house, a place where I had rested on many an occasion. I nodded to Benbow, cocked my leg over the saddle horn and rolled some dusty tobacco shaken from a Durham sack on to a brown Rizla paper. I rolled it, licked the paper and fired it with a blue top. Cigars and stogies were hard to find, as was pipe tobacco, and I quite enjoyed the moment of making the smoke.

It was a peaceful pause, a few moments of concentration on something other than the trials that had beset our long journey south. Benbow did not smoke; he told me that he had once tried it, but it had made his head spin, given him a feeling of wellbeing but had at the same time disoriented him and he had somehow lost a couple of hours.

I wondered just what he had been smoking.

The ranch house was just as I remembered it: single-storeyed, wide and long; built for comfort on money raised by the blood, sweat and tears of rounding up and breaking wild horses. The stone chimney topped one end of a flat-topped roof and the adobe walls stood white and clear. Next to the main house was the five-bed bunkhouse with an outside crapper and wash shack and behind that and a little to the left a cook-shack. The red barn was in need of a coat of paint and the corral was in need of some repair but was stout enough to house the lone pony standing hip-shod in the shade of the lean-to shelter.

The clear-water creek that ran past the house was low, as was usual at that time of the year. Smoke curled from the cookshack's steel chimney and the windmill creaked and groaned in the gentle breeze that rustled the leaves of the stand of live oaks sheltering the small iron fence that kept guard over the graves of my mother and father.

There was no sign of life and I wondered on the whereabouts of old Abraham, my father's right-hand man, a freed slave and a second father to me. I remembered in that moment, as the smoke drifted from my lips, his tears as I left Lazy B and headed off to war.

Washington was buzzing; the dome of the Capitol Building had been stiffened with scaffolding as the hurried work continued to finish in war what had begun in peacetime. The streets were alive with whorehouses, bars and gambling dens. Fortunes and reputations were won and lost daily in the beds and on the gaming tables.

On the stoop of an unremarkable building on a nondescript street a man sat reading a newspaper. On his lap and partly hidden by that newspaper rested a sawn-off Greener; the weapon was at half-cock. Just inside the door and at the bottom of the uncarpeted wooden stairs sat similarly armed men. In a small office at the top of those wooden stairs Major Horatio Vallance was seated on the corner of the desk, studying a large map of the Union coloured in blue and red. Red for the Rebs: he liked the sound of that.

An orderly entered the sparsely furnished office and whispered in Vallance's ear:

'Major E.J. Allen to see you, Sir.'

The colonel got to his feet and shook hands with the man ushered in by the orderly.

He was a tall man with an auburn beard and his words were tinged with a soft Scottish burr. He handed Vallance a yellow sheet of paper.

'This telegram was just now received by our Washington office. It came via San Antonio and Gettysburg.'

Vallance read the telegram and smiled for the first time in weeks.

'Son of a bitch made it – they both did! Now we shall have some fun. When he brings me the head of Buford Post I will put it on a stake, go to Pennsylvania Avenue and parade it around the White House lawn.' He crossed the room to a small cabinet from which he took two shot glasses and a bottle of the very best Scotch whisky. He filled the two glasses and handed one to the newcomer.

'Your health, sir.'

The newcomer touched glasses briefly.

'To you, Colonel Vallance.'

'No, Sir, to you, Mr Pinkerton.'

Both men laughed.

CHAPTER FIVE

TEXAS MY HOME
SWEET HOME

I finished and dogged my quirly, settled back on to the
saddle and nodded to young Benbow to follow me down
the slope to the distant Rocking Lazy B. We walked our
horses across the yard, paused at the hitching rail by the
covered veranda and waited quietly. Benbow looked at me,
an unspoken question on his lips, but I shook my head. I
had seen the shadow by the barn door and had no wish to
be chomped in half by double-0 buckshot from a sawed-off
scattergun toted by a short-sighted old man.

'Can I be of help to you gents?' The voice was almost as
I remembered it; huskier, more tobacco-stained but still
very recognizable. The man was ancient, a man of colour,
wearing a tattered straw hat above a dark face liberally
freckled with dark-brown age spots. A frail man, short in
stature, round-shouldered and in faded and much
repaired dungarees was watching us, a sawed-off ten-gauge
in his hands, both hammers cocked.

'Depends,' I said, half-turning in the saddle.

'Depends on what? You got business here then state it clear. If not, best you ride on.'

'We have a complaint, my *compadre* and I.' I winked at Benbow.

'And that would be?'

'We were camped up the wash last night and that damned creaking windmill kept us awake most of the night, so we came by to grease it for you.'

'I don't hear it, but then I don't hear so well.'

'You don't see so well either, do you, old-timer?'

'Don't give me none of your lip, boy. You be riding on like I told you.'

'I rode a long way to see you, Abraham, but if that's the way you want it, so be it.'

I nodded to Benbow and we reined our horses around to face the old man. He stood there, staring, his rheumy eyes watering, his lips trembling, his hands shaking.

'You take care that scattergun doesn't go off and take your foot with it, you old rascal. I've been shot at enough to last me a lifetime.'

'Joshua? Oh my gentle Jesus, Joshua! They said you was dead but I never believed it, I never. . . .' He dropped the shotgun and was running across the dirt yard to me. I swung out of the saddle and caught him as he fell into my arms and buried his face in my shoulder, weeping as he had when I had ridden clear of Texas and headed north to kill Yankees.

Benbow stepped down, picked up the shotgun, lowered the hammers and took the reins from my hand.

'I'll take care of the horses, Cap, you take care of the old man. I'll catch you up later.'

I had once told him not to call me 'Captain', not to identify me by rank and so he had reduced it to 'Cap'. I let it ride.

*

'You didn't skedaddle, did you, boy?'

The two of us were seated facing each other across the rough timber table in the centre of the bunkhouse in which the old man had been living. We were drinking coffee from tin mugs, brewed in a fire-blackened enamel can. Benbow sat apart in the corner of the narrow room nearest to the flickering oil lamp, reading the book he had been carrying since we left Pennsylvania. I had never thought to enquire as to its title.

'No, Abe, I am still in the army, still a serving officer, working now as a procurement officer for the Confederate Army. My uniform is not needed for that.'

'Procurement officer?'

'I buy things for the army, supplies, horses, powder and shot, stuff like that.'

'A storekeeper?'

'Kind of I suppose.'

'No more fighting?'

'No more fighting, Abe, and no more war; I had a bellyful of that.'

I filled my pipe and passed the pouch across the table to him; he took it and pulled a short-stemmed corn cob out of the breast pocket of his faded dungarees. He half-filled the bowl and carefully tamped down the last of the tobacco that Benbow had rescued from the pocket of the oldest Jayhawker, whom I had killed twice, and lit it.

I waited for the inevitable question. We had just about talked out the workings of the ranch. One horse wrangler, Jerry Jones, had stayed on for no pay, just room and shared board. Sheriff Aaron T. Booker had seen to it that the ranch was off limits to would-be profiteers who were buying up the land for nickels and dimes and lawyer J.T.

41

Everard had seen to it that the money I had left was used mostly to pay the taxes levied by the state to support the war effort.

I waited.

'Did you find them, Joshua? Did you find my boys; are they coming home to be buried where they belong?' He asked the question around the stem of his pipe, the words softly spoken.

In one way the answer to his question was simple: a yes or a no, but there was more to it than that; more was needed from me, much more. I thought about it for a very long moment. I got to my feet and walked over to the open door, I loved the smell of Texas, the smell of the yellow-jasmine-scented night air.

'No,' I said at last, 'there was nothing to bring home. Over four thousand men, brave men on both sides, were killed or severely wounded in that battle the Yankees called Bull Run, many of them are known only to God, buried deep in unmarked graves. Too many. There was no way of knowing where Tom and Luke fell, or even if they were together; cannon fire, bullets, sabres and bayonets scattered their remains far and wide.

'I said a prayer for them – for you, then I moved on. Maybe one day, God willing, I can take you there, show you the field, but it will be a long time yet, I fancy, before the killing ends.'

He listened carefully, drawing on the pipe, staring at the table top. He was thinking, I guessed, remembering the singing and laughter we had all once shared in that very same room with the hired hands, my father joining in and my mother coming over with a platter of hot biscuits, waving away the smoke with her apron and sharing the laughter. They were good times, very good times.

'Maybe they did come home with you, Joshua, you just

didn't know it; maybe they are here with us now, remembering, singing about the Yellow Rose of colour.'

'Maybe,' I said, 'maybe they did.' There were now so many ghosts in my past and I fancied there would be many more before my race was finally run.

The old man got to his feet and tapped the bowl of his pipe empty into the potbellied stove.

'I'll be turning in now; Jerry will be back from town soon. He will be tickled pink to see you.' He walked to the open doorway and paused to say over his shoulder:

'I love you, son.'

'And I you, Abraham Smith, and I you. It is good to be home.'

Then he was gone and I was alone with my dead pipe and a hatful of memories. I remembered my promise to Joseph Morgan; another memory to lay to rest, another promise to keep.

Modesty was around fifteen miles from Pueblo as the crow flies. One morning, when the chores were all done: the repairing of the corral, the greasing of the windmill, the tally of what stock still remained on the grassy range, I would tell Benbow of my promised visit and leave him and Abraham Smith to paint the barn, the last and least appealing of the chores I had set out in my mind for us to complete.

Benbow looked in through the doorway and nodded.

'Buried it in the barn, deep. I will be glad to see the back of it, damned coin weighs a ton.'

I smiled and bade him goodnight.

Later, in the very early hours of that morning when the darkness of sleep was impossible to find, I wondered why I had not asked him about Lorena Booker.

Perhaps it was because I was afraid of what his answer might have been.

CHAPTER SIX

BUFORD POST

Buford Post was a grey man in every way. He wore a grey suit, grey half-boots, grey shirt and tie. His pallid face, seemingly impervious to the impact of the hot Texas sun, was grey. His facial hair was white, his long straggling locks curled over his collar and his grey eyes flashed as he studied the plate of bacon, beans and easy-over eggs set in front of him. Satisfied with its appearance, he tucked the table napkin into his shirt and silently chewed on his first meal of the day.

Behind him in one corner of the room sat Felix Jerome, garbed in a cheap town suit, a battered fawn derby hat over his eyes. From time to time he cast his eyes over the pages of the newspaper that he was pretending to read. Felix was illiterate and his main object in life was to look as inconspicuous as possible as he surveyed the area surrounding his employer for any sign of danger.

In the street doorway of the hotel dining room his brother Harold sat in a tilted-back barroom chair. a sawed-off eight-gauge shotgun across his narrow lap, his busy eyes studying the main street of Bitter Creek for any

44

unseen threat. A stray town dog walked past him, stared at the leg of the chair, thought better of it and moved on.

Harold watched as the telegrapher emerged from his little office across from where he sat and made his hurried way towards the hotel. The little man mounted the board-walk and waited for the nod indicating that he could enter. Harold stared at him, wondering why a man would do such a job, stuck in a little airless office in this Godforsaken burg, hot in his black sleeve-protectors, his green eyeshade and with nothing to show for an eight-hour day other than a few dollars and a sore backside. Harold made more in a week than the telegrapher earned in a month and that, he thought, was the way a man should be.

He nodded. The little man hurried inside and sta-tioned himself in front of Post's breakfast table.

'What is it, Hawkins?' Post asked in a rasping voice, rough but deceptively gentle in its way, with a slight accent, an intonation, Eastern: maybe New York.

'A telegram, Mr Post. . . .'

'Now why didn't I think of that? Thought you might be bringing me some of my special Mex tobacco.'

'That will be Sunday, sir; it always comes on a Sunday, they bring it to the church for you; they only come on a Sunday.'

'I know that, man, I was being . . . oh, forget it. Give me the wire.'

Hawkins drew a yellow envelope from his pocket, handed it to Post and stepped back, waiting to see if there would be a reply. There usually was.

Post took a small silver fruit knife from his vest pocket, opened the blade and slid it along the envelope. He reached inside and took out a single thin sheet of the cheap paper used by the telegrapher. He read and reread the neat pencilled writing then waved his hand to dismiss the messenger, barely hiding the look of satisfaction on his grey face. Hawkins scuttled out, irritated that for some reason he did not get his usual two bits of federal coin for the personal delivery. Northern money was more acceptable and he stored away every nickel he could earn. Confederacy money would be useless when the war was lost – and lost he was sure it would be.

Post looked at the message again; it was brief and to the point.

CSA officer representing army quartermaster arrived in Pueblo. I await your instructions. SB.

About time, he thought to himself, smiling. He screwed up the note, ignited it with a blue-topped match, then lit his cigar from the burning paper. A suitable response would need thinking about; Post was not a man to act on impulse where business was concerned.

Buford Arthur Post was a self-made man; indeed he was more than that, more than a mere man, he was part-octopus with a tentacle in just about every corner of Texas and the southern Mexican border country beyond the Rio Grande. He could handle a gun better than most but he seldom took a life; he enjoyed more the power of paying and watching other men to do that for him. He reasoned that capping a man gave but a singular pleasure, but the pleasure of paying a man to kill, having that power, was more than that gained from doing the job oneself.

The Apache, he knew, believed that they absorbed power from the lives they took, but some believed that that power was doubled if they made another do the killing for them. That was what Post believed, whether it were true or not; many of the things Buford Post believed had little truth in them; they were often the product of his imagination, stimulated when puffing the weed that his only close friend, the Mexican thief Chico Moreno had introduced into his grey world.

Post stared through the smoke of his cigar to where the oafish Harold Jerome sat in his tilted-back chair, nursing the eight-gauge. He wished Chico would come soon so that they could talk, drink and smoke way into the night. He missed the Mexican bandit; they had been together a long time, from their early rustling days of shipping tick-infested cattle across the border, horse-thieving and gun-running. It had been slow but the War Between the States had been a godsend and they had profited mightily from the death and destruction of a country torn apart by a civil conflict that was rending the Union asunder.

Post was of Texas but was not a Texican in the true meaning of the word; he was not a native son and certainly not a patriot. Had he been around at the time he would happily have left the Alamo and Texas to Santa Anna and he could hardly care less about the ideals of Governor Sam Houston and his cronies. Texas to Post was just a big chunk of land, a lot of it pretty and grassed but one hell of a chunk of it mountainous, dry and hot.

Born of churchgoing parents, he had shunned the ministry and when his Baptist minister father had led them from the east coast to the border with Louisiana he was just a kid. He had abandoned them and their damned church as well.

His one aim was to make money, and to make it the easy way by taking it from those who already had it, had done their labour. Rustling had become hard and dangerous work; Texans did not take kindly to having infested cattle driven across from Mexico and the newly formed and

reorganized Texas Ranger companies had made life difficult along the border for Post and his partner Chico
Moreno.

What with the law, the Kiowa, the Comanche and the
Apache life had become pretty well impossible. Then, just
when they thought about moving on to greener pastures,
some fool fired on Fort Sumter and all hell broke loose.
Suddenly, almost overnight, what they had to offer was
much sought after by both the blue and the grey and the
price that the pair set was readily met. The commerce of
war never changes.

CHAPTER SEVEN

MINE EYES HAVE SEEN THE GLORY . . .

Joseph Percival Morgan – strange how I never shortened that name – was, like me, a Texan and, like Sam Houston, he had very deep misgivings about the war. I first met him in '62. We joined the Confederate Army together, he asked me why and I told him it seemed like the right thing to do. I never elaborated on that answer or asked him why he had enlisted. My reasons were much deeper than that, though: I wanted to kill Yankees, I wanted that so bad.

My daddy and my two brothers ran wild horses in West Texas and supplied them to the Confederate Army; it was lucrative and we had fun. My brothers enlisted shortly after the shelling of Fort Sumter and were both killed at First Manassas. My mother died of a broken heart and one evening shortly after her passing, just around sunset, my daddy held me close, kissed me on the forehead, whispered something to Abraham and walked out to our big red barn. I heard the shot and I ran, found him in the hayloft with a single lead ball in his head and tears in his eyes.

I carried that big thumb-buster of a Colt .45 throughout the time I served. I do not know whether or not I ever hit anyone with it before my march up to Cemetery Ridge but it felt good in my hand and that was the last time I fired it: just before I skedaddled.

I met Joseph Percival Morgan, a fellow Texan, when we enlisted and we proudly rode together with Hood's Texas Brigade. We fought our way through those tough early days of war and became good friends, often sharing a pipe and a song. He had a sweet, almost pure voice and could hold any tune, but especially *The Yellow Rose of Texas*, our marching song.

We had our horses shot out from under us at Little Round Top during the battle of Gettysburg. As no remounts were available we linked up with Longstreet's infantry and become foot soldiers for one long and deadly day. Waiting for the order to march, sickened by the death all around us and the stink of our dead horses, I knew I had had enough of soldiering and I told Joseph that this was my last day of war, that if I survived, which seemed unlikely, I was heading south and to hell with Bobby Lee, Jefferson Davis and the whole damned bunch of those who commanded but were not out there on the battle-field, dying with us as we marched, charged or rode into the enemy's rifle-fire and the exploding cannon shells.

As we waited on the order to attack I loaded all six chambers of the Colt with powder and shot, crimped the caps on to the nipples and rested my sabre on my shoulder. Joseph Morgan grinned and stood by my side as we marched up the slight incline towards the waiting Federals. Two canisters exploded near by and he was lost to me in the smoke. I did not pause or break stride but continued to follow the colours up the hill to Cemetery Ridge.

That was the end of my war, or so I thought.

Modesty didn't quite live up to its name. It was a fair-sized township in a large rock-strewn yet green landscape fifteen miles north of Pueblo, settled quietly by a clear-water river of the same name, surrounded by cottonwood trees. It was cattle or horse country, a fertile land.

It was a warm Sunday midday and Main Street was deserted, apart from two dogs, tongues lolling, settled in the shade of the overhead covering outside a general store, and several hip-shod ponies moored to the hitching rail outside one of the two saloons. A bank, a smaller store, a billiard room, a tack room, a large livery stable and a blacksmith's, a government land office, an undertaker and barber shop combined, a town marshal's office, two diners and two hotels made up the bulk of the business area, while three side streets named after Confederate generals tracked to the left and the right, leading to residential areas beyond.

On a slight rise to the north of the town there was a church and a graveyard, the latter ringed by a low iron fence. Several new arrivals sported drooping flowers in rusting tin cans. I dismounted in front of the town marshal's office and ground-hitched the sturdy pinto I had purchased in Dogwood, a small settlement a few miles to the south of Pueblo. I had left the bay that had carried me the long last leg of our journey south to enjoy a rest at the Lazy B.

The office was closed, the door locked.

Too stiff and weary to remount, I led the pinto along the street to the church and tied the animal off to a small rail by the large double-fronted door. The church was freshly painted white and in good repair, with a small steeple sporting a proportionately small bell: small but noisy, I guessed, when ringing clear and calling the faithful to prayer. I removed my hat and beat some of the dust out of my black woollen pants and jacket, wishing I had taken the time to put on the long duster that was tied behind the cantle of my saddle. I removed my sidearm and stashed belt and holstered Colt into a saddle-bag. Then, hat in hand, I mounted the steps. I pushed open the door and stood there for a long moment my eyes adjusting to the change in light. The place was cool, the pews inviting. The plain altar and cross were new, a large Bible stood open on the lectern.

I was not alone. A large man of colour sat in the front row. He turned as I entered; he was wearing a stiff white collar at the top of his dark shirt. He stared at me for a long moment, nodding almost as if welcoming me, as if he knew me, was expecting me. He examined me from top to toe, then, with a wide, white-toothed smile he turned back to face the altar, got to his feet, crossed himself and moved to a piano standing in the corner opposite the pulpit. He was a good head taller than me, six-four at least.

I watched his back as his long fingers ran across the black and white keys. He filled his lungs and in a deep, nut-brown melodic voice began to sing: '*Mine eyes have seen the glory of the coming of the Lord, he is trampling through the vintage where the grapes of wrath are stored . . .*' I sat quietly listening, a pleasurable sound and a long while since I had last heard it, a popular song of the Northern Army. As the last note died he got to his feet, turned to me and smiled that smile again, a tall handsome man.

'Welcome, pilgrim, welcome indeed.'

'Not a popular song hereabouts,' I said, 'Small congregation, or did I miss the service?'

He chuckled, 'You are it, pilgrim, the whole darn shooting match. Small but attentive, I hope, and I don't see why the Yankees should have all the good songs.'

'Why so?' I asked.

'Excuse me?'

'Why the small congregation?'

'New church opened over in Rockwell. They gave me this old one and I painted it up some. Small congregation at the best of times, mostly blacks, but a few white liberally minded Texans do attend. Big wedding over there today, about three miles from here. White preacher; some folk prefer it that way and don't seemingly cotton to a nigger talking to them from a pulpit.'

I shook my head but could not hide my distaste of the use of the word 'nigger'. I studied the lining of my Stetson and said nothing.

'Oh, don't worry, sir. Sticks and stones may break my bones, it is only a word. It is the tone in which it is used that counts.' He laughed. 'What brings you to my church?'

I got to my feet, reached out and took the proffered hand.

'I need some information and the marshal's office was closed.'

'Daniel Preacher,' he said. It was a firm handshake. 'A fitting name: my owners gave it me; ironic, don't you think? They were religious folk, Southern Baptist. Master was a preacher – they never whupped their slaves on a Sunday.'

I smiled. 'The marshal?' I asked.

'Of course. Don Henry Lodge, our town marshal, is over at Rockwell with the rest of them. A strange man, a hard man, but he is easily led, he will be drinking free booze from the wedding cups about now. What information can I give you?'

'I'm looking for a man, an old friend of mine.'

'How would he be called?'

'Joseph P. Morgan by name.'

A frown darkened his smiling face, slowly driving away the friendly gleam in his dark-brown eyes as if a rain-filled storm cloud had suddenly passed overhead, blotting out the sun from the midday sky.

'I know of such a man; I will take you to him.' He moved past me towards the open door.

'Just tell me where I can find him. I am in no hurry.'

He turned to me, 'No, sir, it is best I show you.'

I followed him out of the door on to the boarded porch, then out across the yard towards the graveyard, touching the pinto as I passed. A deep feeling of depression was filling my heart with pain and my head with thoughts of dread. He opened the small iron gate and I followed him across the graveyard on a pathway, mostly lined with board markers, to a freshly turned mound of earth topped by a china vase filled with Indian paintbrush. Their crimson heads made a stark contrast with the white board marker. He stopped, crossed himself and waited as I passed him, walking through his long shadow.

The carved marker simply read in capital letters:

JOSEPH P. MORGAN

1835-1863

RIP

I removed my hat and knelt down beside the grave, bowed my head and closed my eyes. It was a long road back to Gettysburg but I was there in an instant. I could still hear the cannon roar, the cries of the dying, that fearsome Rebel yell of the charging men as they overtook me in their haste to die and always the stink of the black powder and death.

I do not know how long I knelt beside the grave but when I stood erect the preacher was still standing there, waiting.

'Did you know him well?' he asked, his voice quiet, almost a whisper and as if he feared the dead could hear him.

'He was my friend,' I said, 'a very dear friend.'

'When did you last see him?'

'Three months or so ago we shared a pipe in a bloody wood at Gettysburg. I can still hear the thunder.' I walked past him and back out through the iron gateway; he followed, carefully closing the gate behind him. 'How did he die?' I asked.

He turned to face me, a genuine sadness in his dark eyes.

'He was sick when he returned, his stump had not healed, had become infected. It smelled real bad. I got the doc to him but it was gangrene and he died shortly after.'

'How long ago,' I asked.

'Three, nearly four weeks back. Are you Joshua Beaufort, sir?'

I nodded, 'Yes, I am he.'

'Some folk think you are long dead.'

'But not you?'

'I knew better.'

'How?'

He ignored the question, saying, 'Joseph told me a great deal about you, sir, and he left a letter for you: wrote it when he knew his life was finished. I have it in safe keeping; he was certain you would come.'

'Thank you,' I said. 'I promised him that I would.'

'Let me buy you a coffee. I have a small house behind the church. Come.'

The tall man overtook me and I followed him in silence, thinking a coffee would be good.

The coffee was good, damned good. He set a mug on a small table and went into the back room, returning moments later with a narrow brown envelope. He handed me the letter and smiled that sad smile that men of the church rehearse so often for the bereaved, but in his case I thought it to be genuine.

'I will leave you in peace, Mr Beaufort. Call if you need me. There is more coffee in the pot on the stove. I will be back in a while but I noted that some care is needed in the graveyard and I will attend to that now.'

I watched him walk away, grateful for the privacy offered me. It was a long letter and a sad letter, written in a lovely clear hand.

There was more to Joseph than I had imagined.

Hi, Joshua, somehow I knew you would keep your promise so if you are reading this you really did skedaddle. Or is the war over, I wonder? I wonder about a good many things these last few days. The stump never healed, went rotten and the pain is intolerable. Daniel Preacher is a good man and the sawbones did his best but it is just one of those things. Life would not have been good for me, couldn't mount a pony and walking with a crutch was hell. Maybe it would have been better had those damned Yankees finished the job up on that ridge. What a terrible waste it all was. We achieved nothing that day but I guess war is always like that, a waste.

I made a will and have left you my small spread. It is about ten miles to the north of Modesty set in a little hollow with a good-sized bluff at the back of it to hold off the worst of the Texas weather. It has fine grazing and a clear-water stream. You will find it to be an attractive property, I called it Shamrock, seems I have some Irish in me like a lot of folk around here.

The shifty shyster in Modesty, Bob Taggart, has the papers. They were signed and witnessed by a Texas Ranger captain who was passing through so they are solid. Pick them up, go visit, see what you think. I know you have a place of your own in Pueblo but look upon this as a gift to you that you can pass on to someone worthy of it. Maybe you will marry the girl Lorena you told me about so often, have kids of your own, maybe pass it on to them. Who knows?

Don't let the war spoil you, Joshua. I am thinking now of that last pipe we shared, remember it? One last thing you can do for me, visit my grave and sing Lorena for me one more time. Sing it the way we used to sing it around the fire after pork belly and beans. I will hear it.

Thanks for being my friend, may life be kind to you.

It was signed simply: *Joseph*

I helped myself to another cup of coffee and carried it outside, rolled a cigarette, smoked it, dogged it and replaced the cup by the stove. I made my way up to the cemetery where Daniel Preacher was emptying and refilling the cans with wild flowers that he had gathered from around the iron fence. He stopped, looked up and smiled.

'Is all well, Mr Beaufort?'

'My name is Joshua – or Josh – and yes, all is as well as it can be. I have a question for you,' I said, quietly.

'Go ahead, Joshua, I will answer it if I can.' He stood up.

'Do you know *Lorena?*'

'The song? Yes, I hear it a lot.'

'Will you sing it with me over his grave?'

He looked puzzled.

'He asks it of me,' I said, 'and without liquor in me my voice is not something men will gather around to hear.'

He nodded and gave that genuine smile again.

We walked over to the grave of Joseph P. Morgan with its fresh flowers. We stood there, side by side, singing that old song, Preacher in his deep baritone voice and I in my whispered words. It caught me once or twice, but I got through it. I hope he heard it:

Oh, the years creep slowly by, Lorena,
The snow is on the ground again
The sun's low down in the sky, Lorena,
The frost gleams where the flowers have been . . .

'It is a lovely song,' Preacher said as we made our way back to the church. 'Much loved by both sides of this infernal conflict.'

I nodded, still thinking about Joseph Morgan and the pain he must have suffered.

'What will you do now?' he asked.

'Ride into Modesty and sign the papers, check out Shamrock and head for home. I have work to do.'

'Indeed you have, sir, and you need to take care in Modesty.' He stopped and turned to me. 'Buford Post is sometimes there and he is never alone.'

I stared at him, somewhat taken aback.

He smiled and touched my arm.

'Major Allen told me you would be coming to Modesty at some time and spoke of your mission. Any help I can offer you only have to ask, but beware; because of the colour of my skin there is only so much I can do, but there are others in Modesty who know you are coming. Major Allen has a long arm.'

'I should have guessed when you played the *Battle*

Hymn,' I said, smiling ruefully.

'Yes, you should have, Captain,' he answered, returning the smile and holding out his hand. 'Dark days behind us and maybe even darker ones ahead. Ride easy, my friend, ride easy.'

'Thank you,' I said. I untied the tired pinto and swung up into the sun-warmed saddle.

'Go with God,' he said.

I looked down at him with eyebrows raised.

'Can't help it,' he said, from within a large white-toothed smile. 'It's the Godley in me.'

'You a real preacher, Daniel?' I asked.

He only widened the smile; then he turned and walked back into the small church.

CHAPTER EIGHT

LORENA BOOKER

Being the county seat, Pueblo was a substantial town as cattle towns went. There were six smaller streets running east and west from its Main Street, made up of dwellings or warehouses mostly. A fair-sized extension and additional corral ran out back of the Main Street livery stable. Main Street itself boasted two large saloons: the Lucky Strike and the Ace in the Hole, and two hotels, the larger of the two being the Cattleman's Rest. Further accommodation could be found at John Snow's Billiard Room and Lodging House. There was a barber's shop, a dentist and the inevitable gunsmith. A doctor's and a lawyer's shingles hung side by side. There were also two general stores, one of which sold millinery.

The county courthouse, which housed the jail and the sheriff's office, was of white adobe; a naked flagpole fronted the fountain that stood before the entrance. There was also a Texas Rangers office in the building but the Ranger, Sergeant Henry Dade, was rarely in attendance, so vast was his bailiwick and so peaceful was Pueblo that he believed his time was best served elsewhere in the territory.

It was a quiet day and it was raining, the steady shower muddying the street but settling the dust of the long weeks of semi-drought.

Lorena Booker moved about the smaller of the two businesses – both in fact were owned by the mayor, John Snow. She carried pad and a pencil and was going about the weekly business of stocktaking. This, before the war, had been an essential part of her duties as manager of the stores; but the conflict had reduced the number of the town's inhabitants considerably which, together with the lack of funds, had reduced the number of out-of-town visitors from the surrounding ranches.

Lorena Booker was a tall woman, only a couple of inches short of six feet. She was pleasantly if somewhat robustly built, with black hair that matched her almost black eyes and her dark complexion was lightened occasionally by a flashing white-toothed smile. She was undoubtedly a handsome woman and, also undoubtedly, a woman of colour. To the townsfolk of Pueblo she was Sheriff Booker's daughter and both of them were held in great respect. Occasionally, to a visiting cowboy, her appearance was too much of a temptation and many a young cowhand had spent the night in the county jail, nursing a sore head or jaw from either Sheriff Booker's big fist or the long barrel of the heavy Colt .38 he carried as a preferred sidearm.

Lorena looked out of the raindrop-spattered store window and surveyed the empty street. She was wishing she was home making a pie, or just sitting in their parlour reading, or even writing one of the many letters that she sent to the young Texican soldiers, far away from home and dying on the Northern battlefields that bore names

61

she had never heard of: Cemetery Ridge, Harper's Ferry, Gettysburg and Manassas.

A dozen horses, most of them outside the two saloons, stood hip-shod, heads down, water running off their back-side-polished saddles. A tall figure emerged from the courthouse and Lorena watched as her father, wrapped in a yellow oilskin slicker, legged it across the street towards the store. She opened the door and the big man stepped inside. He peeled off the oilskin and a heavy mackinaw and shook his bare head, his long grey hair sending a spray of rainwater across the floor.

He was a sharp-eyed, hawk-nosed, dark-faced, rangy man, into his late sixties but still slim and light on his feet. He wore a big iron on his hip and a silver star, fashioned from the back of long-ago discarded pocket watch, was pinned to his vest.

'Forget your hat, Dad?' she asked, smiling at him, her deep voice tinged with laughter.

'Couldn't find it,' he answered, his own deep soft voice always gave her pleasure. 'Damned if I know where I left it.'

Lorena shook her head in exasperation, went behind the counter and returned with a black, high-crowned Stetson and a blue towel.

'You left it here this morning. I am surprised your head was not still in it.'

Booker grinned ruefully and pulled up a chair beside the black potbellied stove. He felt the coffee pot and tried to hide his disappointment that both were cold. He opened the cracker barrel, reached in and pulled out a handful of the dry white crackers.

'What are you doing? Stocktaking?'

'It's a rotten job but someone has to do it,' she told him.

'I have heard those words a hundred times,' he said. 'I wonder who said them first.'

'Probably a storekeeper,' she said.

'Or a lawman.'

'You want a cup of coffee?'

'Sure could use one.'

'The other stove is on out back. I've just put the pot on; it will be a few minutes. Are you in a hurry?'

'Not particularly.'

Lorena returned to the window. Two cowboys in ponchos drifted out of the saloon, climbed on to their wet saddles, turned their ponies north and headed out, probably broke, wet and hungry. Being a cowboy these troubled days was not what it once had been, she thought, feeling a pang of sorrow for the pair.

'Can we go home and have an early supper, Dad?' she asked, then turned when there was no reply. She stared at her father; his brow was furrowed, his eyes troubled, his fingers were stroking his long moustache.

'What is it, Dad?'

He got to his feet.

'He's back. Josh Beaufort is home from the war. I met Abraham at the livery this morning. He told me Josh has been back for nearly a week. He was as surprised as I was that he had not been to visit.'

Lorena stared at her father, then turned her attention back to the window and the empty rain-swept street.

Supper was a quiet affair; neither father nor daughter wanted to be the first to mention the return of the troubled horse-wrangler who had, on his own admission, gone to war for the sole purpose of killing Yankees.

CHAPTER NINE

MODESTY

Lawyer Robert J Taggart was not hard to find, and was indeed as shifty-looking as Joseph had described him. He was a narrow, birdlike man with a pinched face and large eyes gleaming coldly from behind wire-rimmed spectacles. His skinny body was wrapped in a dark, well-worn frock coat and matching pants. His limp handshake was not reassuring, nor was the look of surprise and concern on his face when I introduced myself.

He quickly glanced at the letter, then reached into a desk drawer and took out a small sheaf of papers. He fumbled with them nervously.

'Forgive me, sir, I was not expecting you. We heard you were dead, killed at a place called Gettysburg.'

'Only the good die young, Mr Taggart. You and I will live to a ripe old age.'

The irony of the remark was lost on the man.

He pulled the sheaf of papers together, his hands trembling slightly.

'You will need to sign the deeds. I will call in my clerk to witness the signature.'

'Thank you,' I said.

'Simply doing my job, sir. Mr Morgan was a brave man and stoic to the very end – a painful end, I might add.'

He called in his clerk and I signed the papers, which he then placed in an envelope and handed to me. I stood up to leave but he waved me back down.

'There is the small question of back taxes on the Shamrock, amounting to three hundred dollars. Can you pay that or would you like time?'

'I'll call by the bank tomorrow before I leave and arrange for my bank in Pueblo to transfer the money to you, then you can deal with it. It will save me coming back this way for a while.'

'But you will be back?'

'Oh yes, I will be back.'

'You have business here?'

'I have a ranch here now; it will need some taking care of.'

'Of course. There is one other thing you should know: should you not want to work Shamrock I have a client who is very keen to buy it and has offered a very fair price, considering.' He rubbed his thin-fingered hands together; he was thinking, I guessed, of the commission he might earn on such a sale.

'Considering what?' I asked.

'The war, sir, the war. Prices are bottom dollar at present but my client is a fair-minded man.'

'And who would your client be?'

'I am sorry, I am not at liberty to say; but trust me, he is reliable.'

'I will think on it after I have seen the place. But for now, thank you and goodbye.'

I left the lawyer's office and stepped out into the hazy late-afternoon sunshine, thinking of my immediate needs and the needs of the pinto. The horse was easy: I left him at the livery with strict instructions that he should get the best: a rub down and good feed. The red-haired kid in charge promised and I gave him fifty cents for the night's stabling and two bits for himself. For me, though, it was a little more complicated; I needed a hotel room, a bath and a hot meal, and then a long sleep.

I dumped my saddlebags on the desk of the smaller of the two hotels, the Drover's Rest, and signed the register, requesting a room overlooking Main Street. The clerk glanced at my signature.

'Is that your Christian name or your rank, sir?' he asked.

I had signed it *Captain Beaufort*, just in case Post was in town and would show an interest in a visiting Confederate officer.

'Rank,' I said and left it at that. The hotel offered a bathhouse out back, so after a long soak and a change of shirts all that was left on my list was the meal and the sleep.

Two eating places were on offer; I chose the busier of the two, Kate's Diner. It was less grand than the other but there were more people dining there, which was usually a good sign since the locals would probably know the best place to eat. The waitress, a handsome, buxom girl with red lips, a ready smile and a red dress, made her way through the crowded tables to mine.

'I can show you a menu but the best thing on it is the beef and dumpling stew.'

She had a deep voice, with just a hint of laughter in it that fitted the smile perfectly.

'If you say so, miss, that will do me fine, along with a large mug of coffee, black.'

'Kate, Kate Ross. Anything else I can do for you?'

'Like what, Kate?' I matched her smile.

'Stranger in town, you might never know unless you ask.'

'You're this friendly to all of your customers?' I asked.

'No, only the tall good-looking ones.'

'Not a lot of them in here this evening,' I said, smiling.

'Wouldn't you just know it, and you being dead and all, you being Captain Josh Beaufort.'

I raised a questioning eyebrow.

'Small town, word travels fast,' she said.

I nodded. 'I do not feel very dead.'

'Some folk were hoping you were.'

'I'm not too popular in Modesty?'

'Not to those some folks. You shoot somebody?'

'Not lately.'

'You did spend time with our black preacher though.'

It wasn't a question; before I could comment she had turned her back on me and walked away. I could hear her deep-throated chuckle. I smiled, thinking: *always fun to haze a stranger*, or had there been more to the approach?

The beef stew was good. I pushed my empty plate to one side and started on my second cup of coffee, I was halfway through it when a shadow drifted across my table. I looked up to see a bulky, moustachioed, middle-aged man in a dark town suit, a narrow-brimmed tan-coloured hat cocked at an angle over his grey eyes, and an elaborate gold-and-silver town marshal's badge pinned to his vest.

'Captain Beaufort, sir?'

I nodded.

'Marshal Lodge: Don Henry, you may have heard of me.' It was not so much a question as more a statement of fact.

'No, sir, I have not, but happy to meet you anyway.' I got to my feet, offered him my hand and indicated the empty chair opposite me. We shook hands, he scraped the chair out and placed his rather large round backside on to it.

I waited.

'Joe Morgan told me about you but I never thought to meet you. Heard you were killed up north somewhere.'

'Seems a lot of people around here heard that.' I looked over to where Kate was moving among the diners, wondering if there was anyone in town other than the preacher, who had not put me down as a dead man.

'I'm glad you made it through. Are you still army?'

I nodded.

'I understand you have acquired Joe's place, the Shamrock.'

Straight to the point. I liked that; no dodging around with small talk.

'News travels fast,' I said.

'Small town, Captain, small town; people tend to live in each other's pockets, it passes the time.' He fiddled with his long moustache.

I waited some more.

'You aim to run it as a ranch, become part of our community?'

Kate came over carrying a large enamel coffee pot. She cleared my plate and, ignoring Don Henry Lodge, asked if I would like more coffee. I said I would and offered the marshal a mug, but he politely declined; he appeared slightly irritated at the intrusion. She winked her eye at me, filled my cup to the brim and left.

'I don't know yet, haven't seen the place. Only found out today that it was mine.'

'It's small but in a nice setting. Difficult to make it pay, I would guess. Old Joe never looked to be in the money – had a few back taxes owing as I understand it.'

'That would be county business, wouldn't it?' I asked. 'Surely not within the purview of a town marshal?'

'I help out the county badge sometimes; he is spread pretty thin.' There was a growing edge of irritation in his voice and he was trying hard to control it, breathing deeply before each sentence.'

'Whatever irregularities there were,' I said, 'I took care of, so you won't be knocking on my door any time soon.'

'That's good to know.'

'I'll take a look at it tomorrow and make up my mind then. I have a spread over in Pueblo County so I am in no hurry.'

He relaxed a little and offered me a stogie which I declined, not liking smoke around me when I am dining in an enclosed space.

'Should you not like it, let me know. I have a potential buyer if you have a mind to sell it.'

'Who would that be?'

I got the same answer as I'd had from Lawyer Taggart.

Marshal Lodge pushed his chair back and got to his feet, lit his stogie.

'Oh, one other thing, Captain. I don't like to see armed men on my street, so you can lose the pistol until you leave my town.'

Then he turned on his heel and picked his way back to the door of the now crowded diner.

CHAPTER TEN

SHAMROCK

Shamrock was as pretty as Joseph had described it, set as it was at the foot of a low red bluff amid a small stand of ash trees, their golden leaves twinkling in the early-morning sun. It was a timber and adobe single-storey flat-roofed building, with a stone chimney at one end, a cold-water well, and a windmill. There came the sound of a small creek, unseen from my viewpoint but running, I guessed, along the base of the bluff. There was also a very large barn, almost out of keeping with the smaller dwelling, and a pole corral holding two horses. A trail of grey smoke was drifting from the stone chimney. I rolled a cigarette and waited, occasionally sweeping the building with my army field glasses, but there was no sign of movement.

It was my ranch; I could see no reason for hanging back so I eased the pinto down the small incline and in to the front yard of Shamrock. The horses in the corral snorted and noisily greeted the paint; almost at once a man stepped out from the building. He was dressed in the usual garb of a ranch hand and wore a sidearm. He was quickly followed through the doorway by a second man, who hung back and leaned on the porch upright, his hand resting on the wooden grips of a Colt.

' 'Morning,' I said touching the brim of my hat. 'It sure is a corker, wouldn't you say?'

'No, I wouldn't say,' the man in the yard said. 'What I would say is that you are trespassing and it would behove you well to move along, pronto.' His voice was morning-thick; probably he was waiting for his first smoke of the day. I could smell coffee in the air.

'Behove?' I said.

'Yes, behove. You know what the word means?'

'I surely do, just a little surprised that you do, is all. Is that coffee I smell?'

'Perhaps you didn't get my meaning? No coffee. Move along is all.'

I looked down at him long and hard, then at the man by the door, wondering which one of them was the faster. I guessed it would be the man in front of me; he had that dropped-shouldered, lean look that goes with a man who is very sure of himself.

'There is something here that needs to be made clear,' I said.

'And that would be?' The man in the doorway now took the conversation over.

'As to just who is the trespasser – or more accurately trespassers – here. It's plural, you see. You do know what *plural* means, I take it?'

He looked puzzled; it was not the answer he'd expected.

'What the hell does that mean?'

'It means there are two of you,' I said quietly. 'This is my spread and you are the unwelcome guests. It also means you have five minutes to get your gear together and ride out of here.'

71

'The hell it does!'

As he spoke the man in the yard reached for his weapon. I drove the paint straight at him. The heavy animal slammed into him, knocking him down with a hefty thump. At the same time I pulled my gun and dropped a round at the foot of the startled man on the porch, who quickly raised his hands.

'You OK?' I asked the man on the ground.

He swore at me. Using the hitching rail as a support he climbed shakily to his feet, looking up at his companion for a lead.

'Sorry, mister,' the man on the porch said, 'we didn't mean no harm. Just looking after the place for Lawyer Taggart. A lot of vagrants pass by here; we didn't mean you no harm.'

'OK then,' I said. 'No harm done either way.' I smiled at the man brought down by the pinto. 'Well, not a lot anyway, and don't you just love the smell of gun smoke in the morning?'

They stared at me, and I wondered what they saw. A man with a gun in his hand was all, I guessed.

'You,' I nodded to the man on the stoop, 'bring a mug of coffee, two sugars if you have any. I'll drink it while I wait for you to clear out. Make it ten minutes. I feel in a generous mood this morning.'

They did it in five. I sipped the coffee and watched as they saddled their horses, tied on their bedrolls and quickly headed out of the yard. They did not once look back.

The ranch house was much as I expected. A small kitchen with a big stove and a sink with an iron water pump took up one end of the dining area, at the other end was a large stone fireplace. There was a nice-sized bedroom and a smaller bedroom with a double bunk in it; that, I guessed, would be for when Joseph needed to hire help. There were also a table, chairs, storage cupboards, an empty gunrack and a back door that led straight out to a two-holed crapper. A typical bachelor dwelling. The stove was still warm, as was the coffee pot, so I refilled my cup and carried it with me across to the large barn.

The building was solidly constructed with a hayloft above the horse stalls; these stretched down one side, giving accommodation for five mounts, but the larger area of the building was taken up by a freight wagon: a new Conestoga, a six-wheeler, six-horse rig. The axles were well-oiled and its large iron-rimmed wheels had been freshly greased. I wondered briefly what the hell Joseph Morgan wanted with such a large rig, then I guessed that maybe it was not his, that he might be storing it for a third party.

It was dark when I got back to Modesty, a low mist was drifting across the landscape, enveloping the town itself. The Main Street oil lamps were flickering in the wind. The scene roused an eerie feeling, one I had experienced before on some distant battlefield long after the cannons had gone silent and the dead had been cleared from the ground. Almost like a ghost, a figure was moving slowly across the street towards me. I reined in the paint and waited as Marshal Lodge approached. The horse was a little spooked but I held a tight rein and he settled. Lodge stopped a couple of feet away and looked up at me, took the wet stogie from his lips and nodded.

'Evening, Don Henry Lodge,' I said. 'Something I can do for you?'

'You've had a busy day, Captain.'

'I cannot deny that,' I said, wondering whether or not

73

to dismount or hold the advantage of the high ground – army thinking was unexpectedly kicking in.

He looked up at me and I was glad I had stayed in the saddle.

'I have had a complaint from a couple of riders that you assaulted one of them and took a shot at another.'

He waited.

I leaned forward and stroked the pinto's neck.

' 'Tis true, Don Henry. Very unfriendly pair; they tried to run me off my own property and I had to persuade them of the error of their ways.'

'You don't say—'

'I do say so, sir, and they were lucky that I was in a pleasant mood today – a mood that is rapidly wearing thin.'

'Is that some kind of threat, Captain?' he asked, that irritation of the previous evening now giving an edge to his voice.

'Don't pick a fight with me, Marshal Lodge; it is not one you would win.'

He reached for the paint's bridle; the animal shook its head and took a step backwards.

'Not a good idea,' I said. 'He does not share my good humour. Oh, and tell that shifty lawyer I don't need anyone watching over my property. I catch them there again they really will have cause for complaint.'

Lodge stepped back. I walked the horse on past him and headed straight for the livery stable, I could feel his dark eyes drilling into my back but thought there was little chance of his following up on the complaints; they were bullshit charges and he knew it.

There was something dark about Modesty, something deeper than I could fathom without gaining more information. One sure thing the army had taught me was that intelligence, information gathered, was everything; any officer, be he a general or a mere captain, acting without knowledge of the enemy's position or intention was likely to be doomed to failure.

CHAPTER ELEVEN

OLD TIMES NOT FORGOTTEN

The morning was cool, the sky a slate grey, but the rain had passed on by, settling the dust and clearing the dry air.

There are some things a man can walk around all of his life and there are some things he has to meet head on. The learning is in the doing, not in the procrastinations of a troubled mind. Although I was not always aware of it, or at least would not admit it to myself, Lorena was one part of my life that I could never forget or ignore for long. She was always there, dark-skinned, dark-eyed, a mysterious beauty, a wraith in the shadows of a memory lost along a trail not taken.

We had been close, almost inseparable, sharing good and bad times both as neighbours and friends, or with me as a sometime deputy watching her father's back, making certain the alleyway was clear of an outlaw's gun or an arroyo safe from a renegade Kiowa. We had been lovers in the truest meaning of the word. But, like most troubled lovers, we had no control over the world, over the actions of others around us, those who held the fate of the nation in their hands. After the cannonade of Fort Sumter, Bull Run and the deaths of my brothers, my mother and father, I had, a slave to my anger, deserted her with parting words now forgotten and, at the time I suspect, meaningless to either of us.

'You ever going to see Miss Lorena again, son, if she knowed you was home?' Abraham was staring at me, his rocking chair stilled, those wet eyes asking me the question that I had quietly asked myself countless times since riding from the valley and heading for the faraway war.

'Mind your own damned business,' I snapped. I regretted my tone immediately as Benbow, who had been sitting on the stoop with us, scraped back his chair and without a word stood up, stepped down from the porch and wandered across the yard towards the red barn.

Abraham looked at me some more; a sadness seemed to weigh him down, to be aging him right there before my eyes. I got to my feet and walked over to him, touched his nappy grey head and stood there beside him.

'Sorry, old-timer,' I said quietly, 'and yes, I am, and this is as good a grey morning as any to do it.'

'Thought it might be, Joshua, I thought it might be.'

Black boots, black woollen pants, crisp white shirt, black vest with the deputy badge still pinned to it and a three-quarter-length vented black woollen jacket all still seemed to fit, although the pants were a little loose about the waist. They were the clothes I had worn as part-time deputy to County Sheriff Aaron T. Booker. I settled the Colt into the high-ride, cross-draw black leather holster, unpinned the badge and dropped it into the vest pocket along with my father's silver pocket watch. I rocked the high-crowned black Stetson a little straighter upon my head over the salt-and-pepper hair, which had been trimmed short, like my moustache, the previous evening by Abraham. Outside the old man had saddled the bay, I took the reins, thanked him, nodded to Benbow, mounted and rode from the yard.

Two hours later I entered Pueblo from the north. The main street was pretty much deserted except for a few hitched saddle ponies and two town dogs, both asleep but with one eye open, stretched out on the wooden sidewalk. Their heads were hanging over the edge, giving the appearance that they should in no way be disturbed but walked around if necessary.

There was a slight chill in the air following the rain, but there was a warm breeze and already the street was drying. A barfly out to earn his two bits was pushing a handcart along the side of the street, his wooden shovel ready to clear the horse-droppings of the previous night. He paused to chat with the lamplighter who, coal-oil can in hand, was checking on the street's dozen or so lamps. They exchanged silent grumbles and parted. All familiar to me: Pueblo, my home.

I walked the bay to the general store that was also home to the milliner and paused there, thinking, staring at the closed door. In my mind I had been through this moment a hundred times; I had wondered, during thunderous days and black bloody nights on battlefields far, far way, around campfires with comrades singing or praying, cowering in holes in the ground, trembling at the cannonade, the grape and the canister, the destroyers of men: what would I say? How would the woman I had deserted receive me? With forgiveness, with warmth, or simply a cold disdain?

For a long moment I thought to ride on by, wait another day or two, maybe hope to bump into her on the street, tip my hat, say *hello*, see what happened. That would only put off the inevitable and that was not really my way. I cleared my right foot from the stirrup and dismounted, looped the rein loosely over the hitching rail and stepped up on to the sidewalk.

Of all of the many fanciful receptions: the good, the bad and the indifferent, I was not prepared for what actually happened.

I was two steps away from the door when it flew open and an angry, handsome, black-haired woman, dark-eyes lit with a yellow flame flew at me, threw her arms around my neck and kissed me hard on the mouth. Then, after taking a half-step back, her hands still upon my shoulders, she said:

'You bastard, Joshua Beaufort! Why the hell have you kept me waiting?'

Then, as she set to kissing me again, I put my arms about her, held her tightly, wanting the moment never to end.

'I am sorry, Lorena.' It was all I could think of to say.

'You damned well better had be, soldier!' Then she was leading me in through the door of the store, turning the Open sign to Closed as we kissed again. I could taste the salt of her tears as I guessed she could taste that of mine.

Much later that afternoon, comfortable in each other's arms on the cot at the back of the store with a couple of preserve jars awash with two glasses of the mayor's finest bottled whiskey, we talked. Talked as if we had never been apart, as if the years of separation were some distant nightmare now past with the beginning of a new day. Neither of us wanted or cared to talk about the past that was yesterday; Lorena's troubled thoughts were filled with the tomorrows of our lives.

'What is going to happen, Joshua?' Lorena asked.

'With what?' I said.

'The war. Will it soon be over and how will it end? People don't talk about it here much,' Lorena said.

'And why is that?' I asked.

'Confusion, I guess. There is still a lot of respect for Sam Houston; people still wonder how Texas got sucked into it.' She stared out of the curtained window, over the distant green grassland of the valley, waiting.

'A lot of folk feel that way around Pueblo?' I asked.

'Yes, they do not speak openly of it; the war is a long way away from South Texas and yet feelings run high in some quarters and silence is preferred.'

'No one knows what will happen but I have seen the Northern war machine close up and the Confederacy cannot win.'

'Can it only lose? Is there nothing in between?' She turned to face me.

'My best guess is that the Old Grey Goose will fight until he is either whipped or dead. And with either his defeat or his passing the South will fall and thousands will die, cities will burn and the end of it will be to fire an unthinkable future hatred,' I replied.

'And our government?'

'They will have very little say; I believe it will be down to General Lee.'

'And you? What of you, Joshua Beaufort, what of you?'

'For the moment I will do what I have to do, right or wrong, to bring this bloody mess to a halt.' As I answered I thought of Vallance and his mission to end the madness as soon as possible and I wondered if it really wasn't already way too late for that.

'Abraham was so happy to see you.'

'And I him.'

'You brought a friend with you?'

'My corporal; he watches over me.'

'Or you over him?' There was the hint of laughter in her deep voice.

'Soldiers,' I said, 'it's what we do, we look out for each other.'

'And is that what you are, what you really are, Joshua, just a soldier?'

I answered her by reaching out for her; placing my hands on her head I pulled her face gently towards mine and kissed her softly on the lips.

Across the empty street from the millinery store Aaron Booker, five times elected sheriff of Pueblo County South Texas, smiled as he watched the pair embrace and vanish behind the closed curtained door. Yet the happiness he felt for his daughter was cruelly laced with an undeniable concern as to her future with Joshua Beaufort; he had a feeling, a worry deep within him that all was not as it appeared to be. He could not for one moment see his former deputy as a merchant for war for either side: not the Federals, who had destroyed his family, nor the Confederacy who, many believed, had fuelled the fire of war at Fort Sumter. Booker had seen the hate and the despair in the man's eyes as he rode away to join the fight, the fight that had turned into a bloody war.

The war was already two years old; those years would not have extinguished that fire.

CHAPTER TWELVE

BOBBY LEE

It was a quiet Pueblo morning; the sun was warm but not burning hot and a light breeze stirred little dust devils, sending them whipping along Main Street. The two town dogs were in their usual place, blocking the sidewalk. I stepped cautiously over them and headed for the Cattleman's Rest Hotel, the larger of the two Pueblo hotels, where I had booked a room, having decided to spend a couple of nights in town. I would read the *Pueblo Echo* in the lobby, then maybe take a quick look-in on Lorena at the millinery shop.

I had just finished a fine breakfast with Aaron Booker; the morning coffee had been laced with sugar and a dash of whiskey. We had talked of old times, leaving the present to look after itself, and I sensed that he had no wish to discuss the war, my being in Pueblo or his daughter's involvement with a Confederate veteran who had left his sweetheart, his friends and his life to follow the Rebel flag for two long years.

His first words had been: 'I see the clothes still fit.'

He shook my hand, a firm grip.

'Where they touch. It's good to see you, Aaron. Been a long while.'

That had been it, like we maybe picked up on a conversation we had been having the day before, as if no time had passed us by. We had shared memories of a gunfight in Del Rio; we had been out of our jurisdiction but we were doing a job that needed doing: taking on three gunfighters as well as the local law, the sheriff and his deputy being totally corrupt. It had been the occasion of my first killing: dropping a back-shooter coming out of a darkened alleyway with a scattergun trained on Booker. It had taken me three rounds to drop the man that first time, but I got better at shooting after that. We had run the local badge out of town and, with the help and backing of the local Texas Ranger captain, had evaded any questions about our right to be there.

The answer to my question about local troublemakers, a frequent pain in the butt to local law enforcement, came when I first heard the name Sonny Blondell. It seemed that Sonny and a few friends were regular visitors to Pueblo, the men being protected by some nameless figure south of the big river. Sonny and his hangers-on would venture out to various townships, cause mayhem, then drift back across the border, any damage being paid for by mail shortly thereafter.

'But one of these days . . .' Booker said, then he left the words hanging and I chose to leave them there, knowing what he meant, what he felt about a corrupt system that had become even more soiled in the absence of the Ranger battalion. Most of the men had heard the Confederate bugles and, like me, had followed their plaintive calling.

'I have known you since you were a dirty-faced kid with a bullfrog under his hat that you used to scare Lorena

83

with. Joshua, you are not here to buy supplies for the Confederacy, you went to fight. The only reason you would quit is you found a greater cause, a better drummer to march to.'

I looked at the man long and hard.

'Can I be of help?' he asked.

'You want to see this war over, Aaron? Finished at any cost and without the mounting loss of life?'

'You are damned straight I do.'

I did not know if it was the right thing to do and I had already hinted to Lorena that things with me were not all they might seem to be. She had accepted that without question, but we were lovers; her father might take a different viewpoint. I gambled that he would not and outlined my mission, omitting Gettysburg and much of the detail.

He listened quietly, then said without hesitation:

'You need my help, you just ask. Texas doesn't need this shit; we're cowboys for God's sake!'

I was halfway across the street when the kid approached me, calling my name.

'Sir, are you Captain Beaufort, sir?'

He was a kid: maybe fifteen, red-haired, lean and hungry-looking. He was leading a tired-looking swaybacked, unsaddled roan on a short halter. The animal had an odd gait and both boy and horse looked about done in. The boy's eyes were red-rimmed and his voice was adult-weary.

'Yes, son, I am he,' I said.

He pulled a crumpled envelope from the breast pocket of his much-repaired and faded dungarees and handed it to me.

'Miss Kate over in Modesty asked me to bring this to you.'

I recognized him then as the young redhead from the Modesty livery stable. I took the envelope from him and nodded towards the roan.

'You rode all the way from Modesty on that sorry animal?'

'Yes, sir, although sometimes when he was real tired I carried him.'

I liked him right off and smiled.

'What's your name, son?'

'Bobby, Bobby Lee.'

'Seriously?'

'Yes, sir, seriously.'

'Were you christened Bobby Lee?'

'No sir, never been baptized or christened.'

I waited.

'Name used to be John Lee but my pa changed it when war broke out.'

I thought about that for moment.

'Where is your daddy now, son?'

'He went to the big fight at Gettysburg and never came back, not yet anyways.'

The big fight? I let it pass.

'OK, Bobby Lee, you take that pony over to the livery and tell the old man there I sent you. Get that animal rubbed down, fed and watered and that front left shoe checked – might as well get them all checked out while you are at it. Then get yourself some breakfast and some sleep. You look about done in.'

'Thank you, sir; we both are.'

I gave him a silver dollar and told him not to leave town without seeing me first. Then I watched as he led the tired roan down to the livery stable, wearily dragging his ill-shod feet through the dust. I wondered what his story was. Everybody has a story.

Even a youngster like Bobby Lee.

In the quiet of my hotel room I opened the note from Kate Ross, wondering what the owner of the diner wanted of me. I was not a bit surprised to learn, when I had read the neatly penned note, that she was in cahoots with Daniel Preacher – and, I guessed, also with Vallance and the mysterious Major E.J. Allen. The note was simply welcoming me as a newcomer to the town and extending an invitation for me to attend the following Sunday's service at Preacher's church, with lemonade and pie afterwards for the whole congregation. I scribbled a note on my CSA notepaper, accepting the invitation, and placed it in the original envelope. I gave it to Bobby Lee early that evening when Lorena and I took him for a meal in the small dining room at the rear of the hotel.

We attracted considerable attention, although no direct approach was made from any of Pueblo's finest, including John Snow, Pueblo's rotund mayor, who nodded politely, tipped his bowler to Lorena and quickly passed us by. The only man to stop, speak and shake my hand was the lawyer J.T. Everard, who asked me to drop by his office in order to sort out some Lazy B business before I left town.

Bobby Lee did not have too much to say for himself but he had a sure-enough appetite. We learned that he lived with his mother in a small town house on the outskirts of Modesty and that she did domestic work for local folk. Although they had had no official word from the army they had been told that his father had likely perished along with thousands of other Confederate soldiers at Gettysburg and would have been consigned to an unmarked grave.

I wondered if Vallance might be able to shed a brighter light on that and thought to ask him when the opportunity arose; it would be a worthwhile thing to do. I could see from the way the boy spoke of his father that he hoped one day to see him walking home along the dusty road to their house. Sad, I thought: there were probably thousands of such children with the same forlorn thought.

In the meantime he was working for pennies at the livery and it occurred to me that maybe, if his mother agreed, he could move down to the Shamrock and keep an eye on the ranch for me. Perhaps he might do a few of the chores, including some repair work that I had noted needed attention. It would keep him occupied and I would pay him more than the pennies he earned at the livery; after all, the money I had was Yankee money, not mine or the South's.

When he had eaten enough for two grown men I offered, at Lorena's whispered suggestion, to get him a room in the hotel, but he insisted that he wanted to be away early in the morning and would prefer to sleep at the livery with the roan – now freshly shod, and be away before daylight. I asked him about breakfast but he simply smiled, rubbed his tummy and rolled his eyes.

Hand in hand we walked him to the livery; I gave him a second dollar and asked him to be sure to deliver the note, said goodnight and watched as he made his way into the dark barn. He was whistling to himself and there was lightness to his step that had not been apparent when he arrived in Pueblo. I promised myself that if he did go to work for me at Shamrock the first thing I would do would be to buy him a new pair of boots.

'I wonder if his daddy is still alive?' I said, turning to Lorena. Then: 'Come, I'll walk you home.'

She stood very still for a moment, staring at me, thinking hard before saying quietly:

'If you still refuse to stay at our house then I am coming back to the hotel with you. You can buy a bottle of wine

87

and we will talk about old times.' Then she was laughing at me: laughing at my obvious confusion.

'People will talk,' I said.

'I hope so. Let's make a noise, give them something to talk about,' she replied.

'And your father, what will he think?'

'Nothing he does not already know. Should he hear anything bad said about us he will probably shoot the gossipmonger.'

'You think?'

'I know,' she said, wrapping her arm tightly around my waist, 'and I will go into the hotel with you, through the lobby, and say goodnight to Benny the clerk. I want to see his face clearly when you order the white wine, chilled and sent up to our room.'

We drank our wine and we sang, as I had sung so many times around a hundred campfires, the softly loving verses of Lorena. We made love and finally I turned down the oil lamps and we slept.

There are many miserably dark nights and hard beds behind me. There is blood on my hands, and once there was a madness in my head, but that night, while I lay quietly in her arms, Lorena soothed me as I recalled, in my deepest sleep for months, my march up to Cemetery Ridge and the horrendous loss of my Brigade companions. I heard again the noise, felt the horror and smelt the stench of human bodies ripped apart by cannon fire.

Moments of such darkness that, thankfully, I knew I would never be able to recall them in my waking hours.

CHAPTER THIRTEEN

LET US PRAY
FOR PEACE

There were seven saddle horses and two ground-hitched buggies in the front yard of Daniel Preacher's small white church when I rode up on the rested bay horse. I tied the animal off at the rail, undid my gunbelt and stashed it in my saddlebag, but I was comforted by the weight of the snub-nosed Colt .36, on loan to me by courtesy of Aaron T. Booker. It was tucked out of sight under my shoulder and hidden from view by the long black Sunday coat I had chosen to wear.

The gun was his personal conversion, five of the six chambers being loaded with paper cartridges. It was his philosophy that if you couldn't get the job done with five rounds then it would be best you didn't get into a fight in the first place. I had smiled at that, wondering aloud: 'but what if the fight involved six men?' His response to that had been to stress the need to line at least one man in front of another, as the pistol was lightly overcharged and would probably go through both of them. There was no gainsaying the logic of that, although I pointed out that it would require considerable cooperation from the men you were facing. He had shrugged.

'If you do not believe they will cooperate then best you don't get into the fight. Oh – and never pull on a faster man.'

The inside of the small church was cool. Daniel Preacher was just about to read from a large black Bible as I entered. I took off my hat and placed it on one of the hooks provided just inside the doorway. I saw only a sprinkling of people: a small congregation made up of four women, several children, and two or three cowhands who were there, I guessed, because they were bored, broke or hungry and the chance of some free apple pie and biscuits made it worth sitting through a sermon.

A few heads turned, gave me a quick once-over, then returned their attention to the covered altar. Kate Ross smiled, nodded and indicated the empty pew beside her, shifting her ample backside along as I returned her smile and joined her.

It was a brief sermon and Preacher's voice was easy to listen to. No fire and brimstone; he spoke mostly about the sadness of the war and the growing need for peace. He made mention of some of the local militia who had gone off to fight and were known to have been killed, and offered thoughts for those at home still awaiting word of the fate of a father, a son or a brother. Everybody joined in a prayer, then he moved to the small piano and, following his lead, the congregation gave a spirited rendition of Rock of Ages. As the singing finished, Preacher turned to face the congregation and nodded his head in my direction.

'I would like to thank you all for your attendance this lovely Sunday morning and take the opportunity to welcome Captain Joshua Beaufort of Hood's gallant Texas Brigade to our community. Joshua was a great friend of our friend Joseph Morgan, late of the Shamrock ranch, who died of wounds sustained at a place called Gettysburg. He has come to our town to pay his respects to an old friend and comrade in arms.'

Heads turned towards me. I stood and, somewhat embarrassed, acknowledged their welcoming smiles.

'Joshua and I have a request to make of you: it is that we sing together for Joseph the song so beloved by both sides in this miserable conflict, *Lorena.*'

He turned back to the piano and the congregation gave a poignant rendering of a shortened version of the song. Beside me Kate Ross gave it her all in a deep contralto voice and I followed along with my whispered version.

Outside in the sunshine the children and the cowhands dug into the apple pie and the chicken sandwiches, while I was refreshed by the cold lemonade served from a cool stone jar. Idle chatter with the locals and some introductions from Preacher saw the lunchtime through, and we had the yard and porch to ourselves as the last cowhand, touching his hat to Kate and clutching a bag filled with pie for bunkhouse companions on some far-flung ranch, rode clear of the yard.

For some reason I made a mental note of the animal's brand: the Slash Y.

'Did you enjoy the sermon, Joshua?' Preacher asked, as beneath the welcome shade of a cottonwood tree we three settled on our cushioned seats in the small porch of the house he called home.

'Restrained, but forceful in its own way. You have a lovely singing voice, Kate; it's a pleasure to listen to you.'

'Are you flirting with me, Captain Beaufort?'

'Stop teasing the man, Kate; we have embarrassed him enough this day.'

The big man smiled, got to his feet and went inside. He returned with three shot glasses and a bottle of whiskey. He set the glasses on to the small porch table and filled each one to the brim. Both he and Kate Ross downed theirs in one swallow while I sipped mine. It was fiery stuff and I had a long ride home ahead of me.

'We have news,' Kate said as she watched Preacher refill her glass. 'Some of it good and some of it bad. There is a man called Sonny Blondell in town and—'

Preacher interrupted her: 'And after this morning's little gathering he will, we may hope, be aware that you are here also. That was the real point of it, although you are always welcome to enter God's house.'

'I have heard of him,' I said.

'What have you heard?'

'That he is trouble with a capital T. A hell-raiser and well protected.'

'Very well protected: he is Post's negotiator. He will set the price for the merchandise you are looking for and it will be a price backed by Buford Post. He is a dangerous man and fast with a gun.'

'Are you good with a gun, Joshua?' asked Kate.

'I used to be a peace officer. I can handle a Colt.'

'There are a lot of dead lawmen out here,' Preacher said, 'and you are not even wearing a sidearm.'

'A lot of dead soldiers also, but I am neither.' I let my jacket fall open to reveal the shoulder-holstered Colt revolver that Aaron Booker had, at my request, loaned me without questioning my need for such a rig. 'Seems your local town marshal frowns on the wearing of sidearms.'

'Don Henry Lodge is in the pay of Post. It isn't too unlikely that you may have to kill him.'

'And I want to be there when you do.' Kate said, giving me a wistful look.

In answer to my raised eyebrow Preacher said:

'Lodge killed her husband, shot him dead and claimed self-defence.'

'He was in the wrong place at the wrong time, probably saw something he wasn't meant to see – I don't know, but I do know he did not even own a handgun, let alone the one found in his hand.' She refilled her glass.

'Local judge?' I asked.

'Studmeyer, circuit judge; he's also in Post's pocket.'

'He is a man with long arms and very deep pockets and I sure would like to meet him.'

'You will have to find some way of getting past Blondell first; either that or really put a burr up his ass.' Preacher smiled. 'I like the latter notion better; the man has had it all his way down here for far too long. Vallance is right: cut off the man's head, the body will most likely die.'

'Vallance said that?'

'Isn't that what he told you?'

'Something like that but not in so many words.'

'How many words does it take?' He refilled our glasses again from a fresh bottle and this time I took the shot in one swallow, wondering if it would not be better for me to stay the night rather than take the dark ride back and maybe fall from my horse. Preacher made up my mind for me though.

'He will approach you here if you are still around tomorrow; or he could follow you back to Pueblo.'

'I wouldn't want that,' I said quietly. 'I will not bring trouble to Aaron Booker and he is on the scout for Blondell.'

'OK then, take a meal with Kate this evening and a room at the Starlight Hotel; it is clean and has a bathhouse in back.' He smiled. 'A hot tub should relax you some.'

He settled himself back into the old rocker that he had claimed for himself, leaving the double swing-seat to Kate and me.

'Where do you think the rifles are?' I asked.

'Near by, or in Del Rio; we think Del Rio. He would need a big wagon to shift that many rifles and there aren't any that would be available to him as I know of.'

I did not correct that thought.

CHAPTER FOURTEEN

SONNY BLONDELL

Daniel Preacher had been quite correct in saying a hot tub would knock out some of the aches and pains that recent activity had saddled me with, and the Starlight Hotel was indeed clean and comfortable. A young Chinaman kept the tub filled with the hot water, which often lapped over the sides of the tub and vanished beneath the boarded floor. Sitting there sucking on my pipe I reflected upon my next move. Clearly I had to check on the wagon in the Shamrock barn; I could do that on my way back to Pueblo. Also I wanted to find out where young Bobby Lee lived and enquire as to his availability as a hired hand and care-taker for the ranch.

Planning too far ahead without more intelligence, though, was futile. I would have to react to any situation that arose and hope I was up to it. Then I remembered Jacob Benbow storming out of the woods with the Remington and firing from the hip. I reckoned we were up to it if we got a fair break.

The price of the tub had been included in the two-dollar room rate so I tipped the Chinaman four bits and thanked him for his service and for dusting down my black suit. He bowed, smiled and left. Back in my room I put on the freshly pressed suit and, almost as an afterthought, packed the shoulder holster into my saddle-bag. I strapped on my cross-draw rig, settling the heavy Colt easily into the greased holster, sliding it along the belt butt forward a little to the left of my belly button. Had I forsaken my army rank and become a gunfighter?

Dinner with Kate Ross was a rather subdued affair, and although I wanted desperately to ask more about the shooting of her husband and the mysterious *maybe he saw something he should not have seen* I left it for another time. We said goodnight and at round about nine o'clock I stood on the sidewalk close by the Lucky Dollar saloon and enjoyed a late-evening stogie. Across the street, walking in the shadows, Marshal Don Henry Lodge passed by on his evening rounds. He looked over in my direction but did not acknowledge my presence.

The inside of the Dollar was the same as that of any other small-town saloon. The bar was long with a brass foot-rail and several spittoons, and the board floor was lightly sawdusted. Sunday evening townsmen wearing suits chattered in small groups; there was a trio of cowhands engaged in a poker game for matchsticks, and one lone man was sitting in a shadowy corner, his back to the wall, a bottle and a shot glass in front of him. He was a big man, as far as I could tell, darkly dressed with a Western-shaped, lightly coloured straw hat tipped over his eyes, making any identification difficult. I could not tell if he was paying me any undue attention.

I ordered a beer, asking for one without a head, and studied the room some more in the long fly-speckled mirror. I wondered why there was always such a mirror in saloons and just how much did such a vulnerable item of furniture cost to ship from the East? I was still wondering that when Don Henry Lodge pushed open the batwing doors and headed in my direction. I watched and waited.

He stood a little behind me and I watched his eyes in the mirror, sensing he had something to say but was just a tad unsure of his ground. I knew such men; there were plenty of them in the army. Give them a rank and they always seem to want to act the part of one rank above the one given. He was a town marshal, nothing more; a constable hired to serve the will of the community, but I doubt he was thinking such thoughts as he stood there, his jacket open and tucked behind his tan leather holster. He was on the prod and I did not turn around.

'I thought I made it clear to you, Beaufort: I don't like to see armed men in my town. I'll not tell you again. Give me that firearm, slowly, and you can pick it up from my office in the morning.'

He was speaking to my reflection in the mirror, not to my back, so I replied in kind.

'Not on your best day, Don Henry Lodge, would a senior serving officer in the Confederate Army of Virginia give up his sidearm to the likes of you.'

The room was suddenly very quiet except for the scraping of chairs as some of the more nervous drinkers got to their feet and shuffled out of the line of any possible gunfire.

His face appeared ashen in the mirror and his right shoulder dropped. I turned quickly just as his hand reached the holstered gun. I smashed a hard fist into his face, heard the nose break, and followed with a fast punch to the side of his head. He dropped like a lead weight to the floor. I stepped over him, moved along the bar and ordered another beer from the startled barkeep, adding:

'And no head this time.'

'Yes, sir, no head.'

All eyes were turned towards me. I heard a scuffling behind and below me as Lodge, blood pouring from his nose, grabbed at his fallen revolver. Before I could pull, the big man stepped out of the shadows, took three quick strides and stamped down hard on the fallen lawman's right hand, loosening his grip on the gun. He kicked it clear across the room.

'No point in besting a rattler unless you draw his fangs, Captain; he will bite you in the ass first chance he gets.' His voice was soft, with a Texas drawl, his smile broad. He looked down at the moaning Lodge but there was no pity in the look and he turned his attention to the barkeep.

'Get him over to the doc's, then take him to the jail and lock him up for the night. Teach him a lesson for picking on the army like that. Hood's Texas Brigade, I hear; he should have known better.'

He offered me his hand, a soft hand; he was no rancher, that was for sure.

'Sonny Blondell at your service.'

The smile seemed genuine and reached clear up to his pale-blue eyes, but you never can tell.

'Josh Beaufort; thanks for the help.'

'Not much help really. I have a feeling you knew what he was capable of and would have taken him. I was just peeved that there was a shindig and I wasn't part of it. You can buy me drink, though, if you've a mind to.'

The bartender pulled a bottle from beneath the counter and poured three large whiskies, downing one himself before moving back along the bar. We drank as we watched two of the poker players drag the half-conscious Don Henry Lodge out through the swing doors and into the dark night. It was a fine-tasting Scotch whisky and I guessed it was not the everyday forty-rod usually sold across the bar.

'They can lock up the town marshal?' I asked.

'If I tell them to they can. When in this part of the country I run my ranch, the Slash Y, and they are a couple of my hands.'

'Saw one of your hands at church this morning. They got religion?'

He smiled.

'No, they got apple pie on a dull Sunday afternoon.' He nodded his head and two fresh glasses of whisky were immediately delivered. 'Let's sit in a quiet corner and you can tell me your story.'

We returned to the shadowy corner and again he insisted on the chair with its back to the wall.

'What story would that be, Mr Blondell?' I asked.

' "Sonny", please. Any story you want it to be; it's a quiet night and I am a good listener. For starters, how long have you known the Negro preacher?'

'Actually, I don't know him. I came down to visit an old comrade's grave and was surprised to find a black preacher here.'

'You shouldn't have been; things have changed quite a piece here in Texas since you left. Many churches in the Lone Star State have slaves as members. Both the Baptist and Methodist. Some slaves have become ministers, but are often still under the protection of masters, who advise and guide them in the ways of Christianity. However Daniel Preacher is a freed man.'

'Protection?'

'Strange world we live in, Captain; not everyone approves of some of the changes, but Texas is and probably always will be a place unto itself. I don't know how we got dragged into the damned war but since we have been we need to make the best of it.'

'He preaches a good sermon, gentle, no hellfire and brimstone raining down upon our heads,' I said.

'I have heard that he does, but I do not care much for churches of any denomination, or to be preached at by a Negro.'

He let the words lie there but I made no comment. He smiled a lot but behind that smile and that disarming manner I sensed a very troubled man: a torn man.

'Who was your friend?' he asked, changing the subject.

'I expect you already know the answer to that, Mr Blondell, so shall we get down to brass tacks and you tell me where my merchandise is and how much we have to pay for it?'

'Why not.' He laughed; it wasn't a question so I did not reply.

'Let's see, three hundred Henry repeating rifles at two hundred dollars apiece is sixty thousand dollars; that, together with two hundred rounds each: say five thousand, brings it nicely to sixty-five thousand dollars, with an option on more ammo if you decide to buy.'

'That is one hell of a lot of money.' I said.

'It is one hell of a rifle,' he replied.

'It is still a lot of money.'

'The price is not negotiable. Not negotiable.' He repeated the phrase just in case I had misunderstood. 'And one other thing, Mexican gold coin, Northern money, silver dollars of the kind you have been spending since you arrived.'

'You don't miss much, do you, Mr Blondell,' I said.

'Sonny – I told you, please, and no, I do not. The war will not be going on for ever and I – we, that is, my partner and I – need to make our price while it is.'

'I will need to think about it and come back to you after I have consulted with my superiors.'

'I doubt that to be true, Captain, but I'll go along with it for a few days. But no longer; the North would be just as happy to have them back; after all, they originally belonged to them. Now, I think I have a date with a bed; can I buy you a nightcap?'

'No thanks,' I said, getting to my feet. 'I need a clear head in the morning, I've a long ride back.'

'Safe journey, then. You know where to find me for the next few days – and oh – watch your back trail. Lodge is going to be mad as hell when they let him out in the morning and he is a back-shooting sonofabitch, take that from me.'

CHAPTER FIFTEEN

BUFORD POST AND CHICO MARINO

Buford Post said, 'Who the hell does he think he is?'

Sonny Blondell studied the grey man over his cup of steaming coffee; other than for the two of them the Bitter Creek Café was empty – empty, that was, apart from the ever-present Felix Jerome sitting in the corner, cradling the eight-gauge sawn-off. Post was scratchy, the result of a night spent with the newly arrived Chico Moreno and a load of fresh marijuana. It was a practice of which Blondell did not approve; it muddled the grey man's thinking and he was apt to act rashly. Business and pleasure, like oil and water, do not mix: of that he was certain.

'I am not sure, Bo, not even sure he knows himself. Part soldier, part lawman, part gunfighter: one thing is for sure, though; if I had not stepped in he would have killed Lodge there and then. I have a feeling he was either baiting the man or waiting to see how I reacted. I also think he had me spotted from the moment he walked into the saloon.'

'Killing Lodge would be no bad thing; the man has ideas above his station and he may need killing before this enterprise is over. He steps on Beaufort's toes again, cap him.'

'It may come to that but for the moment we need him.'

'Do you think the Reb has the money, has brought it all the way from Richmond?'

'Oh, he has it all right; I have seen some of it, freshly minted Northern silver dollars. Looted, I guess, but I suspect most of it is in gold, too much weight to tote this far in silver. Getting him to part with that much cash for merchandise unseen is not going to be easy.'

'If that's a problem then deal with it; this damn war could be over any time soon and those rifles won't sell worth spit south of the border.'

'I have brought them across the border and moved them to Del Rio; yesterday I sent a wagon and ten men to bring them back whenever and to wherever you think best. I'm not sure, but I do not believe he will part with the money without some persuading.'

'Then persuade him; it's something you are good at.'

'He may need to meet with you. He knows more than he lets on is my guess.'

'Then I will meet him; meet him maybe with you, Chico, the Jerome brothers and a few others, take him down, take the money and keep the Henrys.' He smiled as the idea crystallized in his smoky brain.

Bad idea thought Blondell as he left the café. He nodded to the younger Jerome on door duty and headed back to the livery for his horse and the long ride back to Modesty. He did the work, rode the dusty rides on bacon and beans, took all the risks, while Buford Post, the grey man he called Bo simply because he knew it irritated him, sat back, smoked weed and ate healthy breakfasts. He had been honest, though. Captain Joshua Beaufort of the Confederate Army of Northern Virginia was not an easy man to read.

A few minutes after the swing doors had stilled behind the departing Sonny Blondell, Chico Marino stepped out of the small back room and joined Post at the table, where he helped himself to the hot coffee. He ladled in two heaped spoonfuls of sugar; the weed always gave him a longing for sugar.

'Did you hear all of that, Chico?'

The tall, handsome Mexican wiped coffee from his lips and drooping moustache with a spotted bandanna and nodded.

'Mr Blondell seems like a troubled man. Maybe our Rebel friend has him worried but we can take care of that – and him if we need to.'

'I like Sonny; he's reliable up to a point. I keep him on a tight rein most of the time but let him off occasionally to remind the county I am still around and running things. It works well but not so well that he cannot be replaced should the need arise.'

'This is a big deal, Buford, one of the biggest we have had; could set us up for any eventuality, maybe even if the stupid politicians and generals do finally see the futility of the war they so readily squander lives and money on.'

'That won't happen until one side or the other is on its knees. I don't see that happening any time soon. Cannon fodder comes cheap.'

'We will see, my friend, we will see.'

'I don't like the idea of Sonny moving the guns to Del Rio. I have little control down there. I think you should see to it that they are moved nearer to Modesty or even Pueblo, or maybe here in Bitter Creek.'

'OK, I will meet with Blondell in Del Rio and move them to wherever you decide, but Bitter Creek is probably the safest small town and we both have men here. Real problem is getting the good captain to part with the coin.'

'Is it a problem, I wonder? Let's face it: he needs them and knows we can sell them elsewhere; it will be harder but there are many markets for them.'

'Would you meet with him?'

'If it becomes necessary, where is the harm in it? Likely he knows the set-up anyway; they would not send a man down here with such authority were he not well informed. Can't help wondering where he's stashed the money, though.'

CHAPTER SIXTEEN

THE PREACHER

Before I rode out of Modesty I found the house where Bobby Lee lived, and checked in with his mother. She was a woman bowed by work and worry, old beyond her years, who would have found life to be a struggle without a missing husband and a growing boy to care for. She told me Bobby was at the livery, had been there since sunup that morning doing his chores, and would not be home until dark. One long day, she told me bitterly, for a dollar a week.

I outlined my needs on the Shamrock to her and said that I would pay the boy forty dollars a month and found, the usual wage for an adult working cowhand. She burst into tears and I was pleased, feeling that I had lifted, at least for a while, a huge burden from her stooped shoulders. Although she was not aware of it, we had both had our lives altered at Gettysburg. It was a generous offer but it wasn't my money and I reckoned Vallance could afford it.

I picked Bobby up at the livery, offered him the job and he was thrilled. He quit the livery right there and then and, together with two gunny sacks full of supplies across the cantle of the second-hand saddle that I had purchased for the roan, we set out for Shamrock. I saw no sign of Don Henry Lodge or of Sonny Blondell, which was a relief.

Shamrock was as I had last seen it. The door was secure and there were no signs of any visitors, so I guessed that either Lawyer Taggart had taken me at my word or, as the wagon had gone from the barn, interest in the small ranch had dissipated. I rode from the yard, turning once to wave at the boy standing there in his new boots, and headed back to Modesty.

After circling the town I made for the small white church. The yard was deserted. I looked up towards the small graveyard and saw Daniel Preacher tending the over-grown corner behind Joseph Morgan's grave. He saw me, waved and got to his feet. He was smiling that broad, inno-cent, white-toothed smile.

'I heard about your run-in with our esteemed marshal. I think they let him out this morning and he hightailed it over to Dogwood. By all accounts there's a little cantina there, just about big enough for him to drown his sorrows, take up with a poor wretched Mexican woman and feel like a big man again.'

'It was unfortunate but unavoidable.'

'It was no bad thing and Kate was tickled pink. Coffee? I have the pot on the stove.'

'No thanks. I have to get back to Pueblo but I do need to get a message back to Vallance. Use your own words, but the thing is that Blondell says Post wants two hundred dollars apiece for the rifles – that's sixty thousand, and another five thousand for the ammo, and it is *not* nego-tiable. Vallance gave me some show money: some gold, some silver, which I have stashed at my ranch in Pueblo, but nowhere near enough to tempt Post on the deal.'

'Blondell said that? Just came out with it, made the offer, knew who you were?'

'And knew what I was here for. Seems Post has big ears as well as long arms.'

'Damn the man!'

'Blondell wasn't what I expected; He was calm, assured, well spoken,' I said.

'He is a man of many facets, Joshua, and I have seen several of them. He is polite and softly spoken when it is required of him, but underneath, and deep within himself he is a very dark and troubled man: a bigot of the worst kind with no liking or respect for anyone – but especially people of colour.'

'I will bear that in mind,' I said.

'Sixty-five thousand dollars, sweet Jesus!' He crossed himself and muttered something under his breath. 'What can you possibly do?'

'You said something the other day about one way of getting the man into the open would be to put a burr under his saddle, so that's what I intend to do.'

'And just how do you intend to do that?'

'There was a big freight wagon, a six-mule Conestoga in Shamrock's barn. I did not give it much thought at the time, but now it has gone. Where? My best guess is to Del Rio, either to move the Henrys or pick them up.'

'And you will then do what?'

'It will take it a week to get there and the tracks were only a couple of days old, so my intention is to track that wagon, steal it and take the guns. Then make sure that Post knows I did it and that I will pay for them but at my price, not his.'

'Where do you think they are headed if they really are being moved?'

'I haven't the faintest idea, but I guess we can find out

when we find the wagon. I want you to get that intelligence back to Vallance as fast as you can.'

'Just you and Corporal Benbow?'

I nodded.

'My informant tells me Post is still holed up in Bitter Creek, says he has seen his two gunsels, the Jerome boys, around – and another thing: that Mexican friend of his turned up yesterday. My guess would be they will arrange to collect the guns from Del Rio and haul them back to Bitter Creek, where he can protect them. He is a big man in Bitter Creek.'

'You think?'

'That would be my guess again. Only one suitable wagon trail goes by there from Del Rio. It is very narrow in places; we could jump them there.'

'*We*?' I queried.

'Damned right, we! It will be heavily guarded; Sonny has men, real bad men at his disposal – too much for just you and the young corporal'

'We are all we've got.'

'No, you also have me. I can ride hard, handle a gun and shoot straight. I wasn't always a preacher. I will get the message out and then meet you in Pueblo day after tomorrow, early.'

'No,' I said firmly.

'Yes,' he said, with equal firmness. 'Believe me when I tell you, Joshua, that good as you may be, you are not good enough to stop me even if you wanted to.'

I did not doubt him.

After a brief but troubled farewell to Lorena and a long discussion with Aaron T. Booker, in which I convinced him that I would be best served in my enterprise against Buford Post if he remained in Pueblo and watched my back trail, Benbow and I rode south. We rode with our long dusters fluttering in the suddenly dust-laden Texan wind. A mile out of town we were joined by a hard-riding Daniel Preacher. The dark-suited man wore a black duster and a tied-down high-crowned black derby hat. He was astride a large black mare, there was a double-barrelled sawn-off in the saddle boot.

'Black's my favourite colour,' he yelled, as we rode hard, three abreast, to where Benbow had tracked the big wagon the previous evening.

It was *Del Rio*, I thought to myself, and gave the bay his head, *and then, if we were right, Bitter Creek.*

It was an unusually cold Texas evening. The last heat of the day had drifted from the rocks and the dusty soil, leaving a chill in its place that seeped through to the very marrow of my bones. I am not a lover of the cold, and mostly winter is not something I look forward to. This evening I was reminded that, like death, winter was always waiting a little further along the pike. I hunkered nearer to the fire and tossed another log into its heart, sending a shower of sparks into the dark night.

Preacher was asleep and snoring loudly. Benbow gave up trying to read his ever-present book, pulled his blanket up around his chin and tipped the broad-brimmed battered hat with which he had been issued. Its brim was downturned, like he was walking into the wind, folding it down over his eyes.

'You think this is where they will bring the rifles, Cap? Been two days now.'

'I am going by intelligence received, Jake. There's not much more we can do except wait and watch the trail to Bitter Creek.' I answered the question that had also been troubling me.

'You sure that Preacher is on the up?'

'Aren't you?'

'Never met a black preacher before, don't have an opinion.'

'Not too common a practice but many churches in Texas have slaves or freed slaves in their congregations,' I answered him.

'Baptist or Methodist?'

'Both; some even become ministers.'

'Did not know that, Cap.' He pulled the book out from under his blanket, looked at it, thought to say something to me but then put it back.

'What is that book you so hell-fired bent on reading?' I asked; sleep was elusive and I felt like talking.

Corporal Jacob Benbow was silent for a very long moment. Outside of general conversation he rarely made any kind of statement or admission without thinking long and hard about it.

'Uncle Tom's Cabin,' he said quietly and waited, I guess, for my immediate response.

I thought about that, surprised and yet not surprised. I had thought it more likely to be a dime novel about the wilderness, savages and the merits of the slaughter inflicted upon those savages by his brave soldiers in their dirty-shirt blues.

I sat up and pulled the makings out of my shirt pocket, stripped a Rizla and shook some of the dusty tobacco on to it. I rolled a neat quirly and fired it with a glowing twig from the edge of our fire.

'Some folk say that book was the start to this bloody war,' I said.

'Seems unlikely, Cap.'

'Yes, it does seem unlikely; still I am just saying, is all.'

I dogged the smoke and rolled deeper into my blanket.

'Goodnight, Jake.'

' 'Night, Cap.'

Then I started wondering, thinking, as I eventually drifted off into a troubled sleep, where had it all begun? The first shot may have been fired at Fort Sumter but where had that cannon been loaded? That would be for others to figure out; I was just happy to be far away from it and maybe doing something that could hasten the last shot fired.

CHAPTER SEVENTEEN

AMBUSH

Sunny Blondell crossed Del Rio's Main Street to where Dan Henry Lodge stood waiting for him. The marshal of Modesty's nose was swollen and there were still traces of blood on his moustache; his eyes were darkened and bloodshot also, a result of the blow from Beaufort's hard fist. The man would eventually pay for that – both Blondell and Post had assured him of that fact.

'You all set, Don Henry?'

'As well as we will ever be.' The man's voice was hoarse.

'How many men do you have?'

'Eight, not counting the teamster or me. Four outriders, two in back of the wagon, a shotgun on the wagon and Jerome riding drag.'

'And you?'

'I'll be taking point. I know the trail better than most; it's the only one suitable for a wagon of this size. Where will you be?'

Blondell studied the angry man, wondering: was he up

113

to it? He guessed that he was and would put up something of a fight should there be trouble along the way, although he doubted there would be.

'I'll be riding on ahead, double check the trail. Any problems I will come back, else I'm riding straight into Bitter Creek to meet with Bo and see to the change-over there. May have to dog it into Pueblo to seek out the gallant captain.'

'I wish I was going with you, I owe that man.' Lodge spat out his disgust and in his spit he could still taste the blood from his ruined nose.

'You will get your chance.'

'How? He will hightail it out of here back to his soldier friends just as fast as he can.'

'Let me and Bo worry about that, Don Henry; you just get these rifles to where they need to be.'

I climbed up the rocky slope to where Jacob Benbow had stationed himself for a clear view of the trail below. It was hot, the midday sun was burning this part of South Texas dry; the recent rain had been to the east and the escarpment was pitilessly hot, offering very little natural shade. We had found a cave for the horses but it was too far from the Bitter Creek trail to be of any use to us.

I had left Daniel Preacher loafing under a small over-hang; he had draped his duster over a dead mesquite to afford him some shade. I was trying to figure out the man's curious sense of humour in telling me he didn't want to get burnt any blacker by the sun than he was already. There are some people I will love, respect or like but never fully understand; the preacher and my old friend Abraham were two of a kind and I thought that maybe you would have to live in their skins to fully understand the trials of a life that had forged their thinking.

'Anything to see, Corporal?' I asked, squatting on my heels beside him. He set down his book and rested his rifle against the hot rock.

'Nothing so far, although there was some dust about a mile or so towards the start of the arroyo. Maybe a rider – not sure; certainly not enough for a wagon or riders. We should know in a little while.'

He was right in his thinking. Fifteen minutes later a lone rider emerged from the heat haze and passed below us. He was moving at a steady pace, looking to the left and right as he rode by. We hunkered down until he had passed. There was no mistaking the big man.

'Sonny Blondell; that confirms Bitter Creek at least, maybe riding point or just checking out the trail for rock falls or whatever. No dust from a wagon, so I guess he is maybe a day out front. You can relax, enjoy the sunshine.'

'Relaxing is difficult.'

'Are you ready for it, son? Could be anything up to a dozen of them and I am very much counting on you. We will have to take them all out of the game, one at a time if necessary. Are you ready to shoot to kill?'

'Are you, Cap?' He studied me, waiting.

It was a genuine question and I knew he expected an honest answer.

'Shooting a man from cover is never as easy as facing him head on or defending your own ground, but in this case it is essential if we are to succeed.'

'Does it really matter that much who gets these rifles, the North or the South? They will still kill hundreds of men, maybe your neighbours or mine.'

I thought about that for a long moment and wondered how an honest answer would affect the job ahead. But then I thought, to hell with it and looked him straight in the eye.

'These rifles are not going to either side, Jacob, they are going to hell in their boxes.'

'You're going to destroy them?'

'Eventually; that's my intention, every damned one of them apart from a couple each for you, me and the preacher.'

'That will sure as hell brass Major Vallance off.' He smiled at some inner thought.

'Not too sure about that, son,' I said. 'If he was honest with us then I believe he might agree; he may even be expecting it of me and that is why he sent you along.'

'Not such a great judge of character as he believes himself to be then, is he.'

It wasn't a question so I just touched him on the shoulder.

'Maybe we can have a small fire in the cave tonight and brew some Joe.'

Then I turned and made my way back to where the preacher was snoring beneath the shade of his duster.

I was dozing, my back hard against a flat rose-coloured rock. My rifle was protected from the sun under my saddle blanket and my eyes were shaded by the pulled-down brim of my hat. My dust-laden shirt was wet with perspiration. The pebble danced off the rock above me and settled on my chest, I grunted awake, grabbed the rifle and looked over to where Jacob Benbow was signalling for me to keep low. I crawled to his side and he passed me the army field glasses. It had been twenty-four hours since Sonny Blondell had passed by.

I swept the distant dust cloud, focused the glasses and waited, counting, then settled back on my heels, looking at Benbow.

'It's the wagon right enough.' I looked into the distance

again. 'One point rider, two outriders on either side, the teamster and a shotgun guard. About a hundred yards back there's a drag rider. Maybe more in the wagon, impossible to tell.'

Benbow took the glasses and confirmed my count.

'Eight men as far as we can tell.'

'The point man is our friend Don Henry Lodge. This changes things a little. I want him alive; if possible put him afoot – shoot the horse if necessary. Take out the mule-skinner and the shotgun. I will take the two furthest away, Preacher's shotgun would not reach them. He can take the pair nearest.

'If you can take out the drag rider, do it. It will be a long shot but that can't be helped. Anyone climbs out of the wagon, drop them. We don't want to get involved in a gun-fight here – shoot to kill. You sure you can handle that, son? Don't open fire until I give the signal.'

He looked at me for a long moment in that way the young sometimes do look at their elders, picked up his Henry, pretended to examine it and looked at me again.

'I put the wooden end to my shoulder, right? Work the lever and the bullet comes out of the metal bit?'

He backed the words with a wide smile; I shook my head and returned his smile.

'Whatever . . .' I said over my shoulder as I slid down the slope to a position just above the preacher, whispered the set-up to him, then climbed back to the halfway mark and waited.

I let Lodge get past me, then as the wagon drew abreast I waved my hand in the air. The signal was immediately answered by the low, flat crack of Benbow's Henry, the report bouncing around the arroyo sounded as if a hundred men had rallied to my raised hand.

Lodge's pony screamed and fell, throwing the marshal

clear; a second round at his feet sent him scuttling to the shelter of the wagon. He reached it just as the shotgun guard fell backwards into the canvas, blood quickly staining his dirty shirt front. Then the teamster hit the ground behind Lodge and dived under the wagon.

The mules brayed but held fast.

I shot the furthest outrider from his saddle but missed the second, catching his fleeing figure in the back with the third round as he turned his mount away from me. Almost at that same moment Preacher dropped the two nearside riders with a single barrel for each and Benbow dropped the drag rider, who had turned his mount and was heading quickly back the way they had come. He had gone nearly four hundred yards when Benbow dropped him cleanly.

Two men leapt from the wagon, both wildly firing their handguns, having no idea from which direction the attack was coming. I dropped one and Daniel Preacher the other. I raised my hand.

'Cease fire, boys.'

The language of the battlefield came back to me, rolling easily from my dry mouth. My ears were filled with a great roar as the reverberating echoes of the rifles bounced along the arroyo walls and the smell of the black powder laced the hot air. I wished I had remembered to put cotton wadding in my ears to absorb some of the concussion of the gunfire.

'Don Henry Lodge, throw out your pistol or get on with the fight; we don't have all day.'

The lawman staggered out from under the wagon, followed by the teamster, an elderly man who should have stayed at home that day. They tossed their pistols on to the ground and I ordered them both to get down on their knees.

118

Off to my right Benbow walked over to the wounded horse and shot it in the head.

'Sure hated to do that, Cap, poor dumb animal.'

We stripped the dead men of weapons and any identification. Benbow took one of the horses and brought back the drag rider while I made the two prisoners dig shallow graves for the dead men and build a low cairn of rocks over each one. Daniel Preacher insisted on saying a few words over them while I waited impatiently, wanting to be away from that place. We strung their horses out behind the wagon and headed for Bitter Creek, turning hard right well before the town, skirting it and heading out westward on the wider trail that led directly to Pueblo.

I had looked back as we set off. All I could see was a dead horse and a gathering of buzzards looping through the blue sky above the graves. The skirmish had all been over in a matter of minutes but it had resulted in eight dead men and the taking of two prisoners.

We reached Pueblo shortly before midnight and were met by Sheriff Booker and a troubled but happy Lorena.

I pointed Benbow in the direction of the big barn that stood beside the livery. He took over the reins and with Preacher beside him drove the wagon as quietly as possible across the rutted main street and through the open door. The guns could stay there overnight; we could move them to the Lazy B in the morning and hide them in the old mine workings near to the ranch house. I was minded not to destroy them immediately, thinking there might be a better use for those Henry rifles somewhere down the pike.

'Two prisoners for you to hold under my warrant, Sheriff.' I shoved the distraught Don Henry Lodge and the teamster into Booker's path. Then I put my arm around Lorena and we five headed for the jail.

'And what would the charge be, Captain?' Booker asked quietly.

'Gun-running and opening fire on an accredited officer of the Army of the Confederacy for starters.'

'Sounds like a firing squad to me,' Booker said; his hint of a smile was hidden in the darkness from Lodge.

'Now wait just a minute. All we did was to—'

'Shut up, Lodge,' I said quietly. 'You give the county sheriff here a deposition as to where you got those Henry rifles and who stole them and I will see to it there is no drumhead court and you can serve out your time as a prisoner of war.'

CHAPTER EIGHTEEN

COUNTING THE DEAD

Sonny Blondell was hot, dusty and very weary as he entered the outskirts of Bitter Creek and reined in his tired horse in front of the livery stable. He nodded to the livery man, lifted his tired body from the saddle and, trailing his rifle, made his way slowly across Main Street to the hotel. Felix Jerome was seated in his usual place by the door, shotgun on his lap.

Blondell ignored the man's questioning look and walked on through the wide entrance. It was dark and cool inside. Buford and the Mexican, Chico Moreno, were the only occupants of the lobby; the pair stared at him but he walked by and bellied up to the small bar.

'Whiskey, a bottle of the best, cold beer, a pint and don't keep me waiting.'

The bespectacled clerk rapidly produced both beverages. The big man set his rifle against the bar and carried his refreshments across the room to where the two men waited expectantly.

121

'Well?' Post asked, as Blondell settled easily into the armed chair, sighing deeply.

'Gone,' Blondell said.

'Gone? What the hell do you mean by gone?' There was an edge to Post's voice and his red-rimmed eyes burned in his grey face. Blondell guessed the man had been smoking the weed that was so readily supplied by the Mexican.

' "Gone" as in not there any more, "gone" as in "vanished". What the hell do you think "gone" means, Bo? It means just that. Eight graves, a stinking dead horse and a whole lot of "gone".'

'The wagon?'

'I tracked it out to the Pueblo cut-off.'

'And?'

'And then I came here; no point in my riding to Pueblo in the dark and not sure of what I would find there in any case. If it was Beaufort he wasn't alone, there were rifle shells and shotgun husks all over the site. It was an ambush clear and simple.'

'It was the army man for sure, the bastard! Who else would have known about the guns?' Then, answering his own question, 'No one is who.'

Blondell poured a large glass half-full with the amber liquid, downed it and chased it with the cold beer. He signalled to the clerk for a refill of the latter.

'Perhaps we should not have set the price so high; maybe he would have taken a better deal? Hell! Maybe we should have sold a piece at a time to anyone who had the right money.'

'Lay off such talk, Sonny, and concentrate on how we get them back and pay Beaufort off for the inconvenience he has caused me.' Post got to his feet and looked over towards the door where Felix Jerome was sitting. 'Harold dead?'

'No way of knowing who were in those graves. We sent out ten men, so either two got clear and are still running or they were taken prisoner. Of course, I could go out there and dig them all up for you if you are so damned sure-fired curious.'

There was a dangerous anger in Blondell's husky voice that Buford recognized and was always wary of. He needed the man more than ever now, so he took the sarcasm and sat down again, tossing a leather cigar case on to the polished table top.

'Smoke and relax, Sonny. I'll get the clerk to wake up the Chinaman and organize a hot bath and a room. Settle down and think hard.'

Blondell bit off the end of the cigar and much to Buford's hidden disgust spat the end on to the floor. Fine in the confines of a saloon with its sawdust-covered boards but not on to the carpet of a hotel he partly owned.

'How do you hurt a man who does not seem too bothered about his own safety? A man who has probably faced death many times on or off of the battlefield, an ex-lawman who has lived by the gun?'

'You hurt those closest to him, *amigo*, that's how.' It was Chico Moreno who spoke, showing a white-toothed smile. 'That's the only way to hurt a man who has no great respect for the safety of his own life. That's how we would do it.'

Post stared at the Mexican, then shot a questioning look at Sonny Blondell.

'What do you think, Sonny? Is Chico right?'

'Could be. It could work.'

'Then find out just who he does care for and hurt them – not kill them, just hurt them real bad and just enough to get his attention.' He laughed. 'Roll me one, my Mexican friend, and pour Sonny here a drink while I organize that hot bath. Sure smells like he could use it.'

Action, a solution, from nothing to something. Buford Post loved revenge; it was always the final pay-off, the ultimate sanction on anyone who crossed him. Blondell was a gunfighter of high regard; he could take Beaufort – of that he had no doubt – but that would be in the last resort: the final act of the game; first get the man down, then kick him in the head and then, maybe, kill him.

Maybe take on that chore himself. Get what he had been planning all along: get the money and keep the Henry repeating rifles.

It did not take Sonny Blondell long to find out just who did really matter to Joshua Beaufort. Sonny had informants in Pueblo just as he had them in Modesty. First thing he learned, though, was that Harold Jerome was dead, named on a list posted at the County Sheriff's office of the dead men who had attacked a serving officer of the Confederacy. Such news would make a vengeful brother out of a very angry and bitter Felix.

Once he had that information Felix would need watching; he was the sort of man who would rather kill from cover and they needed Beaufort very much alive, at least until they had the money and the Henry rifles in their possession. Then and only then could he – maybe – have the army man. Blondell also learned that the muleskinner had been sent packing with Booker's boot up his backside and that Don Henry Lodge was in custody, rumoured to be awaiting transfer to a Southern Army prison. That last piece of intelligence would most certainly rattle Buford Post more than news of the death of one of his trusted and long-serving bodyguards.

Then there was Lorena, County Sheriff Booker's handsome daughter: from adoption or from a mixed marriage no one knew for sure; all were smart enough not to mention or discuss the matter out loud. Booker was very protective of his daughter and had been ever since the very day he had arrived in Pueblo on a battered, fire-blackened buckboard, toting the baby girl in his arms. He was a lonely man who had taken on the role of father and deputy sheriff; he had been an efficient deputy who was quickly elected as the county badge and he had remained so through many bitterly fought campaigns. Booker was probably untouchable if Post did not wish to bring the whole of Pueblo County down on his neck.

The captain's corporal, maybe? They were close: both were soldiers and would fight for one another tooth and nail, but he doubted that either one would walk away from his given duty to the flag.

The preacher? Now *there* was a real possibility; he and the captain had obviously taken to one another, and although the big black Bible thumper was unlikely to join in any fray he would likely offer support and succour to the military, as that would be in many respects the smart thing to do. Sonny Blondell had never met a preacher who did not have one eye on the collection plate.

Then it hit him. Abraham Smith: the freed black man who had part-raised Beaufort and was one of the reasons, so Blondell had heard, that in earlier days Beaufort had been so reluctant to join the Southern cause, why his family were so averse to slavery. Abolition was not a popular cause in the South but the Beauforts were a fiercely independent family by all accounts. Maybe he was the weak link, the captain's Achilles' heel; everyone had one; he wondered exactly what his own might be but could not think of one. A threat to the Negro just might make Beaufort see sense. It was, he reasoned, worth a shot and he would put the idea to Post that evening.

CHAPTER NINETEEN

ALLAN PINKERTON

I stormed out of Booker's office irritated by the fact that just as Lodge was about to give a deposition to the sheriff implicating Buford Post in the sale of stolen ordnance, the shyster lawyer Bob Taggart had arrived and informed us that his client would not be giving a statement and anything he might have already said had only been offered under duress. Booker shrugged his shoulders and confirmed that the man would be held and charged by the circuit judge, then would be sent to the state penitentiary to await transport to a Confederate Army post for processing. We guessed that Post was behind the appointment but Booker was powerless to do anything about it. He said he would again try to persuade the ex-marshal of Modesty of exactly where the man's best interests lay.

I was just passing the reception desk in the Cattleman's Rest and thinking about a warm quiet evening in Lorena's arms when the desk clerk coughed for my attention, then whispered quietly that there was a man in the room next to mine who wished to converse with me as soon as I returned.

'Describe him,' I said.

'Largish gentleman, foreign, bearded, maybe an Irishman or a Scot, certainly not from around here.'

I thanked him, thinking there was only one man I knew of who even vaguely fitted that description, but he would not be here in South Texas. I knocked on the door of the only other room on that landing, pushed it open, stepped inside and moved quickly to the left, the Colt already in my hand.

'I don't believe you will need that this day, Captain Beaufort,' Allan Pinkerton said, with the hint of a chuckle.

'My God, Major, you are the last person I would have expected this far south of the Mason-Dixon line. Did Vallance send you to see whether we are behaving?'

'The good major does not know I am here – or why; he is far too wrapped up in the drama of his war. Drink with me? I have an excellent bottle of Scotch in my valise, two glasses and a pair of cigars the like of which I am certain you will not find around here.'

I believed him and took one of the two chairs in the room, sighing as I sat down.

'Bad day, laddie?'

'Most of them are these days, Major,' I said.

' "Allan", please; I am not here on army business, nor the enterprise you and the good corporal are engaged in. I am here to see you.' He poured two generous measures and raised his glass to me.

I responded and sipped the smooth drink that had been brewed over a long time in a faraway land.

'Exactly why have you taken the risk of coming down here to South Texas?'

'To see you,' Pinkerton replied. 'My associate Danny Preacher reports very favourably of your actions, although he is a bit vague as to your intent.' He smiled. 'However, to be direct, I like the way you think, a freethinker, outside of the norm, if you understand my meaning?'

I shook my head.

'No matter,' he said, holding his glass towards the window and studying the colour of its contents. 'Sometimes there are things you cannot see, such as how good this whisky will taste, just by looking at them; the hidden things in a man are what really make his measure.' He turned back to me. 'To put it as clearly as I can, I am recruiting for men to join my organization just as soon as I resign my so-called commission with the US Army. I would like to enlist the support of both you and the corporal, who also gets a good report from Danny.'

'There is a war on and I am committed to serve, so any discussion of future employment in whatever enterprise you have in mind is not possible, even if I were interested.' Truth to tell I was very much interested.

Pinkerton laughed a belly laugh, leaned forward and whispered:

'Just between we two, I honestly do not think that Major Vallance is expecting you back once this venture is over.' He straightened and added, 'How is it going, by the way?'

'I have the guns, most of the money. All I need is Buford Post's head, then I can walk away from this charade and get back to wrangling horses.'

He laughed again and shook his shaggy head.

'And you? Did you expect me back?' I asked.

'No. I would not have come here if I could have waited in Washington to see you. But as it happens I am actively recruiting from both the North and the South, I have made many contacts through my work in Washington and I am pretty sure exactly whom I can trust and who may be interested.'

'What exactly is this enterprise, Allan?'

'The Pinkerton National Detective Agency; you may have already heard of it. This war will end sooner or later and there will be many problems and a need for such a group. I foresee a lawless land. Look, Captain, you just think about it: being part of a nationwide private law agency working with the law. Our motto: We *never sleep.* You like the sound of that?'

We talked long into the evening about his dream, the war and even of Vallance's idea of shortening the conflict but, like the bottle of Scotch, the evening came to an end. We shook hands, I promised to think about his offer and looked forward to seeing him again in the future. I kind of liked the idea but there was too much at stake here in Texas for me to allow myself any distraction.

CHAPTER TWENTY

A DAY AT THE ROCKING LAZY BEE

Although the summer sun still burned brightly autumn was near by and the late afternoons and evening had a chill that warranted a log fire. I was chopping firewood in the yard, pausing every little while to help Jerry Jones stack the cords of wood on to a barrow, then stare at the barn while I awaited his return. It did need a coat of paint, sure enough.

Lorena and Abraham were in the house preparing what, judging by the sweet aroma drifting out through kitchen window, was going to be a fine supper. It had been quiet in Pueblo so I had returned to the Lazy B with Lorena. There had been no word or sign of Buford Post. We had hidden the Henry rifles in an old mineshaft that my father had discovered many years after buying the ranch, but it proved to be nothing more than a lot of hard work.

Benbow was out visiting Shamrock, checking on Bobby

Lee, and would be back around eight, in time for supper; no doubt he would be tired from the long ride but he was young and a meal always seemed to stoke his furnace. I was enjoying the late-evening discussions with him, especially when Lorena chipped in with her view of the war although, to be honest with myself, her viewpoint was not one I always agreed with, especially where the barn was concerned.

I stood there, resting on the hickory axe-handle, trying to work out how much paint it would take to protect the old wood for another five or so years.

'What colour are you thinking, mister?' Lorena joined me with a stone jug in one hand and a glass of cold lemonade in the other.

'I'm thinking red again,' I said, sipping the sweetened drink made with water from the wells of home; hard to beat.

'I'm thinking green,' she said. 'Too many bad memories with red, don't you think?'

'Some things need to be remembered; we need to be reminded of the bad as well as the good, else how will we learn?'

'What about white then, a fresh start?' she suggested, taking my empty glass and refilling it from the jug.

'Would reflect back too much heat; you never see a white barn around here. Up north, maybe.'

'Black then?'

I shook my head. 'No, too sombre.'

'You still like red?'

'I think so,' I said.

Lorena gave me that look and shrugged.

'It's your damned barn!' she said as she turned away. 'Paint it whatever colour you want; you will anyway so why did you ask me?'

'I don't remember asking you,' I called after her departing back, knowing that that was not the end of the discussion; just a pause in the negotiation. I still liked red.

'Rider coming in,' she called. I looked to where she was pointing and saw the unmistakable shape of Sheriff Booker emerging from the haze, tall as always in the saddle, a born horseman. He turned his horse in towards the barn and handed Jerry the reins.

'Give him a rub down if the boss can spare you the time.' They both smiled, knowing the answer to that.

He shook off his duster, tossed it on the log pile and gave Lorena a big hug before shaking my hand. I could see he was a troubled man and waited while he drank lemonade from my glass.

Lorena went back to the house to get her father some coffee. Booker nodded towards the barn and we walked a ways together. He stopped short of the wide doorway and I waited patiently for him to speak; he was a man of few words and I knew he was thinking to tell me as much as he could in as few words possible.

'Sent Lodge off as requested with two deputies, Ike and Pete Sloan; you know those boys?'

I nodded.

'Five miles out they were ambushed; five masked men. Lodge ran free.'

'Are they OK?' I asked.

'Both still alive when I left; shot up pretty bad, although Doc Hill thinks they will make it.' He studied the barn some more. 'What colour are you going to paint it?'

'Seems not to have been decided yet,' I said.

'Red would be good.' He smiled at me, relieved, I think, at my reaction to the news of Don Henry Lodge's escape, knowing how much I was counting on using him to pin Buford Post to the wall.

'I'm real sorry, Josh. Maybe I should have sent more deputies with him.'

'Then you might have gotten more men hurt. I'm just happy the Sloan boys will be OK. I've caught the sono-fabitch once; I can catch him again, he won't be too far away.'

'Probably as near as Post and Blondell, wherever they are – and that would be Bitter Creek, out of my jurisdiction,' he said, sadly I thought.

'That used to not to bother us too much, Aaron. Remember Del Rio?'

'And the Rangers – that sure was one hell of a fight!' We both laughed.

'What are you two old codgers laughing at?' Lorena asked, handing her father a mug of dark coffee. 'I put a splash of pick-me-up in that for you, Dad, you look worn out.'

'We were talking about the barn,' he said mischievously, 'I'm thinking red would be best.'

She looked at us, shook her head in disgust and walked back to the house.

Aaron Booker winked at me and we laughed some more.

The smell of cooking supper had truly promised the taste of eating it: rabbit stew with dumplings and greens from my mother's small garden, still tended with great care by Abraham. Benbow had returned with the good news that Bobby Lee was one very happy boy and that many of the chores around Shamrock had been tended to with great care. Better yet, the boy's mother had been out to visit him, driven there in the livery's buggy by an old gentleman friend, and had stayed and cooked a midday meal.

'Looks like they are both doing fine, not having to

worry about each other so much. Good for the boy, good for his mother.'

Lorena nodded approval of the news.

'You have any views on the colour of the barn, Jacob?' she asked him sweetly, looking at me and crossing her dark eyes.

'I like yellow, Miss Lorena, but I think the boss is going for red.'

'Yellow? You are as crazy as he is.'

It really was a fine evening and we sang a few fondly remembered songs while Booker played on my mother's old harpsichord. Booker turned in early as did Benbow. Jerry and Abraham did the dishes and wandered off to the bunkhouse while Lorena and I sat there with our arms around each other and kissed a long kiss. She pulled away from me then and gave me another of those darkly troubled looks.

'Dad told me about Lodge; there is going to be trouble, big trouble; I can feel it.'

'Nothing I cannot handle,' I told her, with just a tad more confidence than I actually felt. I reached for her again but she held me off.

'Promise you will not be killed, Joshua. I would die with you if that were to happen.' There were tears in her eyes and the old song flashed through my head, the familiar words: *The years creep slowly by, Lorena, Snow is on the ground again*. . . . Time, it seemed, was never on my side. I reached over, turned out the oil lamp and there, in the near darkness lit only by the flickering of the sap-laden pine logs, we made love.

CHAPTER
TWENTY-ONE

DARK CLOUDS AND
A COLD WIND

Felix Jerome was fired up with anger, still stinging from his recent encounters with both his direct charge, Buford Post, and his indirect keeper, Sonny Blondell. When Blondell had informed him of his brother's death Felix wanted to ride over to Pueblo and call out the Rebel officer there and then, but Blondell had forbidden him to make any such move. On top of that Post had warned him against taking any action that would endanger their current enterprise, warned him on pain of death, and no one messed with the grey-faced man when he was in that sort of a mood.

Both he and the recently released Don Henry Lodge had been confined to a small line shack on a rundown property owned by Post, where they spent most of their time complaining to each other, devising ways to defy their master by taking out Beaufort, drinking cheap wine and playing poker for matchsticks. None of these pastimes cooled them down or improved their respective moods. At last they reached the same conclusion: Beaufort had to die sooner rather than later at a time chosen by them, not by Blondell or Buford Post.

'We ride into Pueblo,' said Lodge, 'blast him clean with shotguns, just like that, four barrels of double-0. Then we head for the border, ride hard. Are you owed any wages, Jerome?'

'Around a hundred dollars, two months' pay. He can stuff that where the sun don't shine. You?'

'Sonofabitch never paid me a cent, just kept me in the job is all; anything else I earned I stole.' He took a swig from his preserve jar, which served as a glass, and spat it out on to the board floor. 'Maybe stop and get a bottle on the way. I'm tired of this piss.'

'At least you are a free man. I hear an army prison is not a lot of fun.'

'Did you shoot those deputies taking me to the stockade?'

'One of 'em. I guess Blondell took out the other one, or maybe the new boy Harry Benson, or the Mexican. You ever tried that stuff he brings in for Post?'

'No, I never did. You try it?' Lodge said.

'Just the one time they got me to try it. It was like smoking horse-shit, made my head swim and I was sick for two days.' Jerome shuddered at the distant memory.

'You have to steer clear of the man when he is on it. Only Blondell can really handle him then – him and maybe the Mex,' Lodge said. He got to his feet. 'I'm taking a crap and turning in.'

'We go tomorrow?' Jerome asked anxiously.

'Let's see what tomorrow brings, Felix; make it a maybe.'

Talking and planning had calmed Don Henry Lodge down somewhat and he was thinking again, thinking it would not be a fun life on the dodge from Buford Post's long reach with empty pockets and only Felix Jerome as a companion. It might be better to wait out the storm and see what the next few days would bring.

'Damn the pair of them hotheads! Sonny, you keep a tight rein on the pair of them; we do not want to blow this deal on account of a dead bodyguard, although I did quite like Harold; he was better company than Felix. But there it is. Get this deal done and we can get back to normal, Booker has no authority here or in Modesty. He's just a county badge.'

'You got anything to say on this, Chico?' Blondell turned his attention to the quiet Mexican who was now sitting opposite him in the hotel lobby.

'I would dump the pair of them,' Chico said quietly. 'You have any thoughts on where to hurt Beaufort a little?'

'Yes, I have'

'Then spit it out for God's sake, man! Christmas is coming,' Post snapped.

'The safest way to go would be to hurt the Negro, his freed man; he is very close to Beaufort – like a second father or so I understand, raised him high when his daddy blew his own brains out on account of his two younger boys getting themselves blown away at Manassas.'

Post thought about that for a couple of minutes while the two men watched and waited.

'How?' he asked.

'The old man goes into Pueblo a couple of times a week with another Lazy B hand; they have a beer and a meal together. We pick a time when Beaufort and Booker are out of town, rough him up a little, give him a message to

137

take back to the ranch with him "The money or the Henrys".'

'How you going to know when Booker is out of town?'

'That one is easy; this weather he goes fishing for crappies at Spring Water Hollow every Thursday which, it just so happens, is one of the days the old Negro is in town.'

Post was thoughtful again, stroking his grey unshaven chin, thinking he needed a shave and was the barbershop open, but saying:

'And Beaufort?'

'We can check, but most days now he spends out on his ranch with the woman, his punch, Booker's daughter. Can't say as I blame him there.' He smiled at his own dark thoughts but kept those to himself.

'What do you think, Chico?' Post asked.

'Let's get this thing done and head back south of the border for some fun.'

'Do it.' Post said, directly to Blondell. Then, turning to Moreno, he said, 'Get that new man – Harry whatshisname – a shotgun and send him over to the barbershop with me, I must look like crap this morning.'

Quite suddenly it did not feel at all like summer; a cold wind blew in from the east, rattling the barn door and sending the windmill racing. Abraham stepped out of the barn and called over to Jerry Jones that it would be better to work indoors than out and the old horse-wrangler joined him, closing the big door behind them.

'Damned wind, Abe! I can take about anything the weather has to throw at me but not the damned wind. It irritates the hell out of me.'

'Best move out of Texas then,' the old Negro offered, knowing, understanding just how his old companion felt. 'Got a jug of medicinal cider back here. Guess we should take us a glass.'

The two old friends settled themselves on hay bales and sipped from their preserve jars, happy in the shelter of the barn listening to the windmill; it needed more oil but that would be a job for a younger man; maybe get Benbow up there as he was the one who complained most about the crying of the metal on metal.

'You seen the boss this morning?' Jerry asked.

'He and Lorena left early for Modesty; gone to see the preacher man.'

'Wedding?'

'No, business more like; he's going straight back to Pueblo. We'll see him in town tomorrow, we'll take young Benbow with us, buy some red paint.'

'You read the paper this week, Abe? Things are looking dark for the South. Lee seems to take one step forward and three back. Too many dead boys; so sad.'

'I'll see it in Pueblo tomorrow if the rain holds off.'

Jones was an avid reader and knew full well that his friend struggled with the written word.

'Lincoln still not had the vote on emancipation so I sometimes wonder what the hell they are fighting for,' he said.

'If they be fighting for me I wish they would stop. Too many young men have died already. My boys – they were the first to go, my boys. . . .'

So the old man's mind wandered off, back to memories of children on his knee, when every day was a sunny day, a time where there was no darkness, no Texas northerlies to cover him in dust. A time when horseflies did not bite and there was just enough rain to keep the grass green for the remuda.

Jerry Jones had heard it all before but listened anyway, sitting there sipping his cider, knowing he would likely

hear it all again the next day when they were seated in the
Ace in the Hole playing a day-long game of dominoes or
checkers.

Late that same night Sonny Blondell rode into Pueblo,
stabled his animal and booked his regular room in John
Snow's Billiard Room and Lodging House. The window
overlooked Main Street; he would see the departing figure
of Aaron Booker with a small picnic basket in one hand, a
fishing pole in the other and a wicker creel over his shoulder. He would watch the man ride clear of the town,
letting him know that the game was on.

It could be fun; he had no love for the blacks be they
slaves or freed men, but he could make an exception for
Lorena Booker. He thought about that as he poured a
measure of whiskey into his glass, kicked off his boots,
stretched out on the bed and turned down the oil lamp.
He was soon asleep, lulled by the rhythmic clicking of the
billiard balls in the room below.

CHAPTER TWENTY-TWO

DEADLY FIRE

Lorena said, 'I like Pueblo and being near to Dad, but I sure could get used to living out there on the Lazy B.'

A few words, gently spoken, that somehow made me very happy. We had not discussed our future together since I had been back but at that moment those words made it seem like a good time to start thinking about it: about life after Buford Post. Following my talk with Allan Pinkerton I had already made up my mind that I would not be returning to the future that Vallance envisaged for me; the job in South Texas would either get done or be left as it was. The rifles were out of the fight and I could send the money back with the young corporal if he decided to return.

As for Post, I guessed he was maybe sulking, ready to count his losses and head back south of the line. Staying would only cause him problems and those problems would likely increase his losses. Should he stay, then there would be a fight, but one I thought we could win.

Lorena and I were talking about this over breakfast in the hotel when I heard gunfire in the street: a single shot. I got swiftly to my feet.

'Your father?' I asked.

'Thursday, fishing at Spring Water Hollow.' She sounded anxious.

I moved quickly towards the door.

'Where are you going?' Lorena asked.

'Stay here,' I snapped back. I felt a great heat inside me, a sense of foreboding that I had no real cause to feel.

I stepped clear of the doorway, glad I had strapped on my gun that morning.

Abraham was standing tall, defiant in the middle of Main Street. My wrangler, Jerry Jones, was down in the dust, resting on one arm, the other arm was holding his head. Abraham was staring up at Sonny Blondell, who had his back towards me, a smoking pistol in his hand.

'Tell your boss he owes me or the next one goes through your foot. See if you can dance then, old man. Tell him, he doesn't pay up you will be one dead nigger. Lincoln wants to send you back to Africa or wherever the hell it is you people come from. Sounds like your best bet if you have not left when Bobbie Lee kicks his ass.'

Abraham looked in my direction and shook his head.

Blondell froze.

'Why don't you tell me yourself, Sonny, and stop beating up and scaring old men?'

'You got a gun on me, soldier boy?'

'I will have if you don't drop yours and turn around real slow,' I told him.

'I guess I'll just have to shoot the nigger,' Sonny Blondell said.

Like Daniel Preacher had said, it was just a word, a common enough address, but at that moment the word

142

filled me with a cold and dangerous rage.

Abraham stared, wide-eyed but seemingly unafraid of the gunman.

'Don't,' I said – whispered the word, really.

'I'm leathering my piece, soldier boy, and turning around.'

Sonny holstered the Colt and slowly turned to face me. He grinned at me but his hand was still round the butt of his pistol and somehow I knew his intent. I pulled and I pulled fast. I shot him through the right elbow. As he jerked away, dropping his pistol, his lips framing a scream I shot him again, this time through the right knee. He went down, moaning, his left hand not knowing which wound to clutch in order to stem the most pain.

A young man standing on the veranda to his left reached for his gun even as I turned towards him, my own Colt still expelling black powder smoke from the fired brass.

'Don't,' I said, this time not in a whisper. The kid froze but I could see in his eyes that he was thinking, wondering.

'Forget it, kid. Not even on your best day with a Spanish angel on your shoulder, not in this world.'

The kid relaxed and walked to the moaning Blondell.

'What is your name?' I asked him.

'Harry Benson.'

'You ride for Buford Post?'

He nodded.

'Go get a wagon, Harry. Get Blondell there to the doc, then get him home and out of Pueblo. I see either of you here in town I will shoot to kill. Oh, and tell your boss: if he ever threatens one of my people again I will send him to Hell on a black horse.'

Benbow was suddenly on the street with us, the Henry in his hands, his shirt tails flying. He stared at me long and hard, then went over to Abraham and steadied the old man, whose feet were shifting to the beat of some unheard distant drum. Abraham was much shaken but was otherwise uninjured. Gripping Benbow's arm with one of his and Lorena's with the other, he wobbled somewhat unsteadily over to me. He looked up at me, then watched as I punched the spent brass from the Colt, reloaded and holstered the weapon with a slightly arrogant flourish.

The four of us stood there and made no effort to help the kid as he loaded the moaning Blondell on to a livery buckboard and drove it off down the street past the gathering crowd of worried onlookers that was dribbling out on to Pueblo's usually quiet Main Street.

'You didn't have to have done that, Joshua, that was cruel.' There was sadness in the old Negro's deep-brown voice.

'He was going to kill you,' I said.

'He mightn't have; maybe he was just sounding off. He is nothing and "nigger" is just a word.'

'Not a word I care for or want to hear, old man, not when five hundred miles from here thousands of men are dying, fighting for God knows what, other than the right for your people to be free.' There was anger in my voice, a touch of despair – or was it shame?

'My people?'

'Yes, Abe, your people: people of colour.'

' "Your" people?' he repeated. 'Are we not all one people? Even you, Joshua Beaufort, do you, like that evil man, see us as a different people?'

'To hell with it!' I snapped. 'Your people, my people – what the fuck does it matter? Next time I will let him or someone like him blow your brains out.'

I rarely curse but something within me was changing and maybe not for the better. I turned to Benbow.

144

'Get him and Jerry over to the saloon, Corporal. Buy them a drink.' I turned my anger and attention to one of the bystanders. 'You,' I said, 'get the sheriff from wherever the hell he is.'

The bystander was a young man in a shabby but serviceable town suit; he was pale-faced and shaking as he stepped back into the small but swelling crowd; I guessed, from the tone of the angry man who was standing in front of him, that he was wanting their protection.

'Sheriff Booker is down on the Hollow, fishing for crappies.'

'Find him for me, son.' I tried to let some warmth back into my voice as my anger subsided a little. 'Ask him to ride out to the Lazy B when he gets back and to bring a couple of crappies for supper; will you do that for me, son?'

The youngster relaxed. 'Yes, sir, I surely will, I promise.'

I nodded, touched his shoulder gently as I walked past him and followed Benbow, Lorena, Abraham and the limping Jerry Jones to the Ace in the Hole. I was wondering what had become of me, to wound a man so cruelly – even a man like Sonny Blondell – and feel absolutely nothing.

I did not like the way that both Lorena and Benbow had looked at me as they turned and, pushing their way through the muttering throng of people, had headed in the direction of the saloon.

That night a dry dust storm, unusually heavy for that time of the year, blew in from the south and covered the Lazy B and the surrounding countryside with a fine yellow powder. The force of the wind was such that it cooled my anger, confined me to the ranch house and mostly to my own company. Benbow had remained in Pueblo with the

145

two old men and Lorena wanted to be alone. Booker, I knew, would not ride out in such a storm. The dust would remain for a few days before a sweet Texas rain would follow it in and wash the land and buildings clean again. I wondered: would it be so easy to wash away my growing anger and frustration with some of my fellow men, not only enemies but also those whom I held dear, who so easily acquiesced and accepted their lot.

Late afternoon on Friday, when the storm had subsided along with my anger, Sheriff Booker rode into the yard and walked his horse to the hitching rail in front of the ranch house. I met him on the porch, we shook hands and he followed me inside. He placed a brown-paper parcel on to the table.

'Crappies as ordered, sir.'

'You had breakfast yet?' I asked.

He shook his head and settled wearily into one of the large leather chairs that my parents had hauled from Virginia and carried with them the long way south by covered wagon.

'Sorry I missed the fracas yesterday; picked a sure-enough day to go fishing.'

I smiled down at him. 'I did OK without you this time around.'

'Took care of one of my problems as well, but I can't help thinking it might have been better had you capped him permanently. You going to cook those crappies for a late breakfast?'

I put some grease in a skillet. When it was spitting I tossed the brace of flour-dressed, gutted and scaled fish, their bellies stuffed with herbs that Lorena had picked and dried, into the hot fat.

We ate the fish with sourdough bread and butter and

washed them down with whiskey-laced coffee. I tossed the bones into the trash and the dishes into the sink. Then we drifted out into the cool evening, sat in the two rocking chairs and filled our pipes. We spoke very little; it had always been that way between us, a perfect trust so necessary when your lives depended on each other's actions and awareness.

Such had been the life of the lawman back in the early frontier days, and we both knew they were not much safer now. We both knew full well it would be worse when the war was over and homeless, hopeless men who had known little but the killing of their fellow countrymen for however many years it might be, would wander the land searching for the lost years of their lives and finding very little to replace that loss.

'Blondell is out of the game for sure; you crippled him good. Buford may move on but I doubt that he will, he still has a base and some tough *hombres* backing his play in Bitter Creek. He will be a burr under my saddle for a long while.'

'And what of Lodge?' I asked.

'He has either run or will run; you scared the crap out of the man in threatening him with a firing squad.'

'That was you, as I recall,' I said.

He chuckled. 'OK, whoever it was. Are you heading back to wherever you came from now, or what?'

'No, I am staying here in Pueblo County. I have had a job offer of sorts; can't say exactly what that is at the moment but it will be in law enforcement.'

'And your corporal?'

'Benbow? He must make up his own mind, but I do have a feeling that although he disapproves of my actions in many ways, he knows we make a good team.'

'Anything else likely to influence your decision?'

I detected a note of amusement in his directness.

'Well, sir, I was hoping to marry your daughter if she will have me.'

'She's mad at you right now, but it will pass; she's waited two long years. I believe you're OK there so long as you don't paint the barn red.'

'I cannot promise that.'

We sat there for long while in silence and I knew there was something the lawman either wanted to tell or ask me, so I refilled my pipe for the third time and waited.

'Josh,' he said at long last, 'I want to clean out Bitter Creek. I don't want that hanging over my shoulders for ever. What are your thoughts on that?'

'Out of your jurisdiction, way out. Or do you mean we do it like old times, like Del Rio?'

'Yes, just like Del Rio; when a job needs doing best to get it done.'

'You know the Vivaldi county badge?'

'Morton Guthrie? He won't give a damn; too far for him to ride, anyway. Old Mort likes the quiet life.'

'Leave it to me then. I will set it up, end this thing once and for all,' I said.

'Just like that? How?'

'Post wants my head and I want his; let's give him the chance.'

'You have resources?'

'I have a good man I can call upon.'

'It's late,' he said, 'I think I will stay the night. You got another jug?'

CHAPTER TWENTY-THREE

THE END GAME

I found Daniel Preacher in the church graveyard, his back to a board marker, an open book settled on his lap. His dark eyes were closed behind his wire-rimmed glasses, a slight wheeze was coming from his open mouth. I opened the creaking iron gate and he snapped awake, looked up at me, shading his eyes from the afternoon sun.

'Oh, it's you, Joshua. I've been expecting you.' His round face brightened as he cracked that familiar white-toothed smile at me.

'Could have been Old Nick himself,' I said.

He thought about that for a moment.

'Maybe it is, I hear you've been a-reaping. You want some coffee?'

'No thanks,' I said, 'had one with Kate in town, had some business I wanted to discuss with that shyster lawyer of Buford's but he was conveniently out of town. Gone to Vivaldi on business as I understand it.'

'He won't find solace there if that's what he's looking

for. Old Mort Guthrie couldn't give a damn about Blondell being all shot up.'

'Word travels fast around here,' I said.

'Just as fast as a horse can carry it.' He grunted, removed his spectacles, placed a playing-card marker in his open book and, with a stiff groan, heaved himself to his feet.

I studied the board that he had been resting against. *Elijah Coombs 1790-1860. RIP*, it read. He followed my gaze.

'Never met old Elijah,' Preacher said, 'but I have a feeling he wouldn't mind my resting on him, I am told he was an ornery seventy-year-old sonofabitch and fell from his horse after a long night in the saloon. Let that be a lesson to us all.'

'And that lesson would be. . . ?' I asked, following him out through the gate.

'Horses and whiskey do not mix when you are seventy years old.'

We settled on his small porch, shaded from the sun by the tall cottonwood tree.

'Did you meet with Pinkerton?' I asked.

'Yes, as did you also, I hear. What do you make of the man and his grand idea? He offer you a job?' he asked.'

'He did.'

'You taking him up on it?'

'Thinking on it,' I said. 'And you?'

'Already have. I sold my soul to that man years ago, right before the beginning of the war, and I have not changed my mind. This will be a lawless country for a long while and lawmen will be needed more than preachers, even black ones.'

'Sheriff Booker and I need some help,' I said, changing the subject, feeling a little guilty about discussing my future with him before letting Lorena in on my plans.

'You want to clean out Bitter Creek,' Preacher said; it was not a question.

'Once and for all, put Buford Post in the ground, permanently.'

'You can do that?'

'We can, with a little help.' I said.

'And that help would be?'

'Three good men and you with that scattergun should do it.'

'And your plan is?'

'Not too much of a plan really. I call him out; he is evil and he is proud, he will say yes and make sure he has plenty of men to back up his play. We will meet and you, Booker, and my corporal and another three will shoot up anyone gets in the way. Cut off the head, the others will flee and Booker will forcefully persuade the county sheriff to appoint a decent deputy to Bitter Creek.'

'And that's your plan? Not too much of one as I can see. Why call him out? Why not just ride in and shoot them all?'

'I have my reasons,' I replied, irritated by his questioning but aware that he too would be laying his life on the line, as well as those of his friends.

'Would old-fashioned pride be one of them?' he asked.

I ignored the question and asked one of my own.

'Can you help or not?'

Getting word to Buford Post presented no difficulty. I walked the hitching rail line outside the Ace in the Hole until I found two ponies carrying the Slash Y brand; one of them was a sturdy pinto. I went inside and asked who owned the paint horse. One of the two young cowhands propping up the bar turned around, gave me the once-over and said, with an edge to his voice, 'I do. What's it to you, old-timer?'

His companion, a rider whom I recognized as the one at the church service, whispered something in his ear. The youngster's attitude immediately changed; the edginess was lost, to be replaced by a nervous smile.

'Nothing much, son, but I have a message for your boss. You give it to him from me, Captain Joshua Beaufort of Hood's Texas Brigade, and you get it right, word for word.'

'Yes, sir,' he said, suddenly eager to please. 'You can rely on me, sir, you surely can.'

CHAPTER TWENTY-FOUR

GUNFIGHT IN BITTER CREEK

'Would you believe that, Chico? The man's called me out. Calls me a worthless bunch of crap and threatens to kill me and sends the message back with one of my own hands. Kid nearly shit himself telling me, repeating what that damned Reb said.'

Buford Post drew deeply on the weed-filled cigarette that Chico Moreno had rolled for him; he was greyer-faced than usual and his eyes were red-rimmed from lack of sleep. 'Is he out there, can you see him?'

'The man said he would be here at ten o'clock, so I guess he will be somewhere out there.' The tall Mexican walked to the hotel barroom's batwing doors and looked out over them into the dry and deserted Main Street of Bitter Creek. Deserted, that was, apart from the tall man standing in front of the livery stable.

'He's standing over by the livery. Wasn't there just now.

Where the hell did he spring from?' Moreno wondered out loud.

'Can you see his sidekick or that black bastard of a preacher?'

'No.' The Mexican shook his head; again he searched to the left and right of Beaufort. 'No, he's alone, the street is deserted.'

'You sure he's alone?'

'Looks that way.'

'Don Henry Lodge, Jerome and the other seven men will be close. Are they in position?'

'Three on the roof, one in each alleyway across the street from here. Lodge and Jerome with two more are out back of the livery, watching the street just in case he has help coming.'

'No worry then; we probably won't need them. Is he wearing a sidearm?'

'A single Colt, butt forward in a belly-draw rig, and I can see a shoulder holster with what looks to be a cut-down revolver in it. Mean-looking sonofabitch.' He stepped back, away from the entrance. 'How do you want to play this – straight on? Or you want me to go upstairs with the shotgun, distract him?'

'Not on your life, Chico. Man comes to my town and calls me out he's a dead man.'

'You high?'

'A little.' Buford giggled. 'It may help, give me an edge. I can shade Blondell so I can sure as hell shade the soldier, but if he gets lucky take him out. Bastard cost me a lot of money, I want his hide for that.'

'No bother, Mr Post, no bother at all.'

'Then let me get it done.' He scraped back his chair and got to his feet. He drew his ivory-handled Colt con-version, checked the load, then dropped it back into the holster; it settled easily into the oiled leather. He stepped out on to the boardwalk and down on to the street, took two steps towards Beaufort, then stopped.

We grouped two miles into the scrubland north of Bitter Creek: me, the corporal with his Henry, Booker and Preacher both carrying sawn-off twelve-gauge shotguns and the three men whom Preacher had drummed up; two of them also carried shotguns, the third carried a Henry rifle. Where he had got that from I could only guess. They looked more like farmers than gunfighters to me, but Preacher assured us they were all dependable and trust-worthy, giving me no reason to doubt their combined ability. They certainly looked mean enough in their wide-brimmed hats and soiled dusters, and no doubt shotguns would be the better weapons in a closed situation like a town's main thoroughfare.

Booker then swore us all in as deputies for the County of Pueblo. It gave us no authority under the law in Vivaldi County, but that was about as legal as he could make it.

The idea was simple enough. They would all drift into town from different directions and, well before daylight, station themselves where they could each cover a section of the ground near to the livery stable. Booker had drawn a map of the town and all were familiar with it. The only weak spots were the roofs and Booker made sure that the shotgunners were clear about covering those.

Accuracy was not as important when clearing a roof as when it was shooting, man to man, on the street below. Two loads of double-0 buckshot could clear a lot of timber as well as doing considerable damage to anyone hiding behind the thin pinewood false-fronts.

I rode the pinto horse into town just before ten o'clock,

walked it through the open door of the livery, dismounted, shucked my duster, checked my weapons and stepped out on the street directly facing Buford Post's hotel.

I waited a full two minutes before the grey man emerged.

'Been waiting for you, soldier. What kept you?' His voice sounded a little odd but it was his moment in the sun so I did not reply.

For all his wealth, his well-tailored clothes, his crooked empire, his fine horses, his power and his bombast, at heart Buford Post was nothing more than a two-bit gunman who liked the sound of his own voice.

'I could have had you killed any time I wanted, Beaufort, but it was not something I wanted to share.' He spoke slowly, enjoying the moment, then hawked and spat into the dust. 'You crossed my path every whichaway, cost me a heap of money, Yankee dollars that will take me a long time to recoup. You are one—'

I had heard enough, I pulled easy, without warning, and shot him in the chest. The round rocked him back and into the hitching rail. He was held there, a look of absolute surprise and disbelief on his face, then utter disgust. His pearl-handled revolver was still in its tooled holster.

'You bastard.' The words were little more than a whisper hardly audible above the metal upon metal as I cocked the Colt and fired again.

That second round jolted him backwards against the weathered wood and he bounced forward, falling to his knees, that look of surprise and despair carved ineradicably on to his grey face. I cocked the Colt, raised it to fire again, but he shook his head from side to side, staring up at me, the light slowly fading from his empty eyes. I gently lowered the hammer.

Then there came a sudden awakening of the grey eyes, a look of incomprehending shock and fear. I wondered what Buford Post was seeing in that final moment: a gathering of devils or a host of angels? I doubted it was the latter, but then again I wondered which he would have feared the most.

I did not wonder for many seconds. Suddenly gunfire of every description burst around me. Screams, the sounds of splintering woodwork, yelling and confusion filled the air. For a moment I was back at Gettysburg and very afraid. Then I came back on the street and into the fight. I went down on one knee, my Colts in my hands both firing.

At the precise moment when I dropped to one knee Chico Marino stepped out on to the street, stared down at the body of his late friend and raised his Greener to the hip, only to be blown backwards through the swing doors by two rounds of double-0 buck from Daniel Preacher's own sawn-off; he was firing from the hip as he emerged from the gloom of the livery stable, a little to my left. Benbow was clearing the alleyways with ten fast rounds from his Henry, and two of Preacher's men were taking the rooftops, blowing great chunks of wood from the cover of the hidden gunners. Two stood clear, tossed their guns down into the street and raised their hands high; both men were bleeding, either from wood splinters or buckshot.

Booker was with me; we stood there back to back, taking down anything that moved. Then, as Don Henry Lodge fled past me on my still-saddled pinto, I dropped him with my last round.

I got to my feet just as the elder Jerome stepped clear of the alleyway, his shotgun at the ready, but a round from Benbow's Henry chewing the woodwork at his feet changed his mind. He dropped the gun and ran off down Main Street. Benbow fired again, kicking up more dust at the heels of the unemployed bodyguard as he cleared the town line, still running. The young corporal stepped clear of the livery.

'Reckon he will be in Mexico pretty soon, Cap.'

'He's probably already there, son. Thanks.'

'You are very welcome.'

I pulled the cotton wadding out of my ears, as did Booker, hoping the others had thought to do the same; the reverberations of gunfire in such a closed-in area can do a man's hearing a whole lot of damage.

Booker looked at me.

'Just like the old days, Deputy. Just like Del Rio.' He whooped and laughed.

Daniel Preacher joined us.

'Short and sweet. Lodge is dead and so is the Mex; five others dead and one pony hit by a stray in back of the livery. Three walking wounded taken down to the doc's.'

'Did we lose anyone?' I asked.

'Not so much as a scratch between us. I'll organize the undertaker and assure folks it is safe out here on the street.'

'Tell them it is all over,' I said, thinking to myself that it really was.

'Are you really going to send his head back to Vallance?' Benbow joined me and nodded towards the prone and very dead Buford Post. The grey man lay stretched out, face down in the bloodstained orange dust of Bitter Creek's Main Street, his revolver still in its holster.

'I don't believe we will, I don't have the stomach for that sort of thing, but we will call on the *Echo*, get their man to photograph the body and send that instead.'

'What about us? Where do we go from here, Cap? Back

to the war?'

'I don't think we will be doing that either, Jake. Pinkerton told me he is quitting the White House and building up his own detective agency. He hinted that he needed men down here and I am pretty sure Vallance would agree, so perhaps we will serve out our time and the war here in Texas and maybe help old Abe paint the barn.'

'And Lorena?'

'Lorena can choose the colour – just so long as it's red.'

We both laughed as the tension and uncertainties of the past four months drained away.

EPILOGUE

In the end three happenings helped to define my future. With her father's blessing, Lorena and I were married by Daniel Preacher at his little church in Modesty in the month following what became known as The Gunfight at Bitter Creek. Jacob Benbow and I – with the complete approval of Major Vallance – began our lives as Pinkerton agents, working for the agency that would become internationally known as 'the agency that never sleeps'.

Later I signed Joseph Morgan's spread over to Benbow. The young ex-corporal would make a good neighbour and the irony of a Yankee owning his old ranch would not be lost on Joseph, wherever he might be.